FRIEDRICH CHRISTIAN DELIUS

*TRANSLATED FROM THE GERMAN
BY JAMIE BULLOCH*

Peirene

Bildnis der Mutter als junge Frau

AUTHOR

Friedrich Christian Delius is one of the most critically acclaimed contemporary German writers. He was born in 1943 and lives in Berlin and Rome. His first poetry collection appeared in 1965. Since then he has published fourteen novels, five poetry collections and has recently written the libretto for the opera *Prospero* by Luca Lombardi. His books have been translated into seventeen languages.

TRANSLATOR

Jamie Bulloch has been working as a professional translator from German since 2001. His most recent works include *The Sweetness of Life* by Paulus Hochgatterer for MacLehose Press and *Ruth Maier's Diary* for Harvill/Secker.

MEIKE ZIERVOGEL
PEIRENE PRESS

I was simply enthralled by the structure of this narrative; a single 117-page-long sentence with a beautifully clear rhythm. At the same time it's a compelling and credible description of a "typical" young German woman during the Nazi era. If we can relate to her we come close to understanding the forces that were shaping an entire generation.

First published in English in 2010 by
Peirene Press Limited
17 Cheverton Road
London N19 3BB
www.peirenepress.com

Reprinted 2010

Originally published in German as
BILDNIS DER MUTTER ALS JUNGE FRAU
Copyright © 2006 Rowohlt · Berlin Verlag GmbH, Berlin

This translation © Jamie Bulloch, 2010

This work has been translated with the financial support of the
Goethe-Institut through German Foreign Office funding

Friedrich Christian Delius asserts his moral right to be identified as the
author of this work in accordance with the Copyright, Designs and
Patents Act 1988

Printed in Great Britain by T J International, Padstow, Cornwall

ISBN: 978-0-9562840-0-6

Designed by Sacha Davison Lunt
Photographic image: Tim Flach / Stone / Getty Images.

FRIEDRICH CHRISTIAN DELIUS

TRANSLATED FROM THE GERMAN
BY JAMIE BULLOCH

Peirene

Portrait of the Mother as a Young Woman

For U.B.

Walk, young lady, walk if you want to walk, the child will like it if you walk, Dr Roberto had said in his funny German with a strong Italian accent,

and, as always when she set off on a walk or to get some things in town, these words that the doctor used to say after her weekly examination, with his persuasive but friendly smile and in that silky voice, danced around her head,

beautiful lady, young lady, healthy lady, moving good, straining not good, and there is nothing more better in Italy for you and the child than the oxygen in the Roman air, and all this for no money, the city of Rome she is glad to offer you and the child her good air,

curious words of encouragement and irritating compliments which were already there before she took her first step outside, as she combed and plaited her hair, and put it up in a bun in front of the small bathroom mirror, then with a sceptical expression put on her only hat, a black one with a broad brim, and stroked both hands over her large bulging belly, and could not find anything about herself that was beautiful besides this belly, because when he called her *beautiful lady* it made her blush each time, in spite of his friendliness and assistance, the doctor had no right to call her that, only he did, her husband, whose return from the African front she had been waiting for week in, week out,

and she tiptoed across the terracotta tiles in the hallway, it was still siesta time, back into her room which she shared with another German woman, whose fiancé had been interned in Australia and who, although almost thirty years old, was known as "the girl" and who worked in the kitchen and helped serve meals, Ilse was still lying on her bed, reading after her siesta,

while she, the younger woman, put on black lace-up shoes, fetched her dark-blue coat from the wardrobe, cast an eye over her bed that had been made and the table that had been tidied and found everything in order, said *See you at supper!*, shut the door, and walked past the bathroom towards the lift and the main staircase

in the centre of the five-storey building, a hospital and old people's home run by Evangelical nuns from Germany, with a few guest rooms, one of which she was sharing with Ilse until the birth, then afterwards she had been promised a room on the fourth floor for herself and the baby,

in this mission, run by the deaconesses of Kaiserswerth, she had everything she needed and it cost her very little, a doctor and obstetrician, a midwife, sisters, regular meals, a bed, a chair, a small table, a drawer for the letters from Africa, half a wardrobe, a tiny mirror in the bathroom three doors down, a prayer each morning before breakfast, a terrace on the roof in a city where, in spite of the frequent sirens, no bombs fell, and where the winter was a mild affair, predominantly sunny and warm,

and placed her hand on the banisters, here she was surrounded and cared for by ten women in dark-blue habits and white bonnets with frilly trims and bows under the chin, stiffened by Hoffmann's starch, one of the sisters was in charge of the kitchen, one the laundry, one the ironing press, one the nursing, one the administration, and the most marvellous of them all, Schwester Else, was in charge of the entire deaconesses' mission, and they all devoted themselves to the patients, to the mothers with their babies on the maternity ward, here she felt in good hands and was endlessly grateful for everything,

especially grateful that they spoke German here, and that she did not have to make any effort to speak a foreign language in a foreign place, which she would not have been able to do, trained as a kindergarten teacher and housekeeper, she felt she had no gift at all for languages, she had not even learnt a handful of words of a foreign language, although she had got the best marks in arithmetic and gymnastics, at school and in the Hitler Youth's League of German Girls she had channelled her curiosity towards biology, to native plants and animals, but never to languages, and thus from morning to night and also now, as she carefully went down the stairs, she blessed her luck

that she was on a German island in the middle of Rome, where even the Italians spoke German, sometimes it was a funny German like Dr Roberto's, sometimes broken like that spoken by the women in the kitchen, but it seemed to her that all of them were making an effort, either because they really liked working here with Protestants, or perhaps because they themselves were dispersed Italian Protestants, brave Waldensians, or because they enjoyed German order or pious orderliness,

and she walked down the stairs, holding on tightly to the banisters, until she reached the entrance hall where three narrow armchairs and a table stood outside the doctor's consulting room, and a vase which always contained fresh flowers, today it was mimosa, three bunches of delicate, yellow, January mimosa, and after going through the glass door entered the front hall with a bench and the tiny room for the reception sister, as they called this post in the mission, usually it was Schwester Helga who was in charge of the key and the telephone, delivered post, showed patients to admission, completed the register, and was the person who had to be informed when leaving the house and the care of the ever-obliging, ever-smiling deaconesses,

it was already three o'clock, the afternoon rest was over, and Schwester Helga was coming to do her warden's duty, she knew, it had already been discussed, that the young woman would go alone to the concert at the church on Via Sicilia, and would be accompanied home through the dark streets by two sisters,

particularly as it might be a few minutes after half-past five, when no lamps shone and windows were covered for the blackout to hoodwink the bombers who had yet to drop a bomb on Rome, and the holes and paving stones on the pavement were hard to make out,

See you at supper! said Schwester Helga, *See you at supper!* the young lady said, stepping through the door, and waited for a moment on the top step, as she took her first breath outside on this bright January afternoon,

Dr Roberto was quite right to praise the Roman oxygen, this air was good for her, the sunlight was good for her, the afternoon sun shone on the right side, her side, of Via Alessandro Farnese, dabbing a little of the precious sun on her face, and making her raise her head so that her hat cast no shadow on her skin and, smiling, she walked past agaves and rhododendrons, up six steps and turned left,

something she could not have imagined nine weeks ago, turning into a Roman street, all alone on a Sunday evening, so confidently and almost without trepidation,

it was nine weeks ago that she had arrived in Rome, so as to be with him for a while at last, with Gert, for the first time since their wedding, and when, the very next day, he had to tell her that he had been ordered back to the army, a sudden, immediate *redeployment* to Africa, and she had not been able to understand,

only just arrived and immediately alone again, highly pregnant in a dangerous, foreign place, it was a shock, at twenty-one almost herself like a child that cannot walk without help or stand on its own two feet, exposed in a totally alien country and a totally alien language,

she looked up past the beautifully moulded window arches and the green shutters of the house that had, years ago, been painted rust-red, up five storeys to the railings of the terrace, searched for the window to her room and, as if it might do her some good, looked with modest pride in her newly acquired cosmopolitanism at the palms in front, which she loved to write about in her letters, all in all a stately building, surrounded with beautiful plants,

her beloved husband could not have sought out a better refuge, she could not have found a lovelier German island, and the child inside her stirred at these thoughts, she stopped, felt the movements of the little legs and arms, she took this as a sign of consent and responded by slipping her right hand under her coat and slowly stroking her dress and the curved belly,

and, as the kicking and punching abated, she began her walk to the other German island, the church on Via Sicilia, where the concert was to start at four o'clock, it was the trusted route from one island to the other, as the rest of it, the immense city of Rome, still seemed to her like

a sea which she had to cross, checked by the fear of all those things unknown, of the yawning depths of this city, its double and triple floors and layers, of the many thousand similar columns, towers, domes, façades, ruins and street corners, of the endless number of pilgrimage sites for cultured visitors, which she walked past in ignorance, and of the faces of the people in the streets, which were difficult to make out, in these stormy times of a far-off war which was drawing nearer every day, but where there is fear, faith can help, she could rely on this knowledge, for the Bible was also a help against the opaque, uncanny sea named Rome, for example a verse from Psalms, cited during morning prayer, *If I take the wings of the morning, and dwell in the uttermost parts of the sea, even there shall thy hand lead me, and thy right hand shall hold me,*

as soon as she recalled this verse she felt comforted and guided and held, and with the encouraging words of Dr Roberto, *Walk, young lady, walk,* and the certainty of being in exactly the right, the most secure place between the African coast, where her husband was serving, and the Baltic coast, where her parents lived, she quickly reached the first street corner, crossed the junction, stayed on the sunny side, looked at the houses in this area, all of them in those friendly colours which had become familiar to her, between bright ochre and dark, faded and washed-out red tones, three- or four-storey high, bourgeois houses, some with thick black arrows pointing to the nearest air-raid shelter, and a few paces beyond the second crossroads lined with ilex the street opened into

the square whose name she had never been able to remember properly, Cola di Rienzo, that is what was written on the stone plaques on the corners of houses, some prince or politician, she had immediately forgotten what Gert had told her more than two months ago, she could not retain all these foreign names in a foreign tongue, it was difficult enough to interpret the gestures and looks of passers-by,

and difficult enough to pull the right face while passing the queue at the bakery, it was shortly after three, the *panificio* opened at half-past three and shut, like all shops, at half-past five because of the blackout, a few women were standing on the pavement, as they always did in the morning or early afternoon, she sidestepped them and continued on her way,

flour was scarce, bread was scarce, it cost three lire per kilo, sometimes all they had was yellow corn bread, and *last spring*, Ilse had said, *they lowered the daily ration from 200 grams per person to 150, two or three slices, and this for the Italians who are used to fresh bread every day*, bakeries had not been allowed to sell cakes and biscuits for more than a year,

again she thought of how fortunate she was, provided with everything she needed, not starving, and not having to queue like the Roman housewives or their maids, how lucky she was that at this hour she was able to go to church, and even to a concert, and was only vexed for a second by the question of

why there is not enough bread in wartime, and why it is getting ever scarcer, seeing that ever more land is being conquered and ever more victories are being reported, after all the wheat is still growing, and the rye, you can see from the window of the train how all the fields were blooming and ripening, so where is the bread, but that was not a question you could ask, it was a test, it was God's will, he provided the daily bread and allocated it,

while these women stood there and looked relieved that she was not queuing up too, a woman eight months pregnant would be entitled to go right to the front of the queue, and that would have made the wait for the few grams of bread even longer, the semi-hostile glances became almost friendly when they realized that she was continuing to the corner of Via Cola di Rienzo,

where before turning left she looked over to the right, to where St Peter's and the Vatican were only a quarter of an hour away, she did not want to go there now, she was not going to be sidetracked, she had been there once before and seen the Pope on the Feast of the Immaculate Conception, together with Ilse she had stood in a crowd of thousands and watched

as the man venerated as the Holy Father sat on a splendid chair and was carried through the church while the mass of people greeted him with rapturous applause as if he were a victor in the Olympia film or the Führer in the weekly newsreel, and she watched the cardinals walk up and down singing, although the huge din meant she was unable to hear any of the singing or prayers, everything seemed so heathen, so loud, so superficial, more like the theatre than Mass and, as she had not understood anything anyway, and did not like crowds, especially not now with her round belly, they went outside into St Peter's Square and Ilse had sighed *Thank goodness for Martin Luther!*, she had thought something similar too, but had not dared utter it, Ilse was generally quicker to say what she thought, and the two of them agreed how lucky they were that they were Protestant and were able to forgo such ostentation,

and whenever she caught sight of the imposing dome of St Peter's, either from the terrace of the deaconesses' mission or while walking through the streets, she felt pity for the Catholics who were intimidated by this mass of stone, who once inside this marble fortress became extras, ants, and subject to an apparently infallible pope, it was said that there were four hundred churches in Rome, each one more beautiful and magnificent than the next, but only one of these was the right one, the church in Via Sicilia, and now she turned

left towards the bridge over the Tiber, walked over the unintelligible letters SPQR, and the intelligible ones, GAS, on the manhole covers, past the black arrows pointing to the nearest air-raid shelter, and narrow shops that were home to a hairdresser and poultry dealer, and which were closed in the afternoons, and past the wall-newspapers that were pasted to a house,

she walked this path almost every day, and sometimes, although this was increasingly seldom, when the dealer had fresh produce to display, gutted, bled and plucked chickens would hang head down in the window, right next to reports of victories in newsprint which was still damp with paste,

there were shortages of everything, of bread, meat, paper, it was thus practical to paste up the papers for all to read, *Notizie di Roma*, the headlines in bold type, mainly consisting of the words *vittoria* and *vincere*, announced victories or the exhortation to victory, wherever one came across propaganda the words *vittoria* and *vincere* leapt out urgently in black,

she was happy that she was unable to read any of it, and did not have to, even in Germany she had not read the papers, it was better not to know too much, not to say too much, not to ask too much, one always heard bad news soon enough, and the only good news came in letters, anyway, especially now that things did not look so good for the Germans and Italians in Russia,

the victory slogans could be heard and read more and more frequently, but no doubt that was necessary, even she thought it necessary, one had to believe even more in victory now, she desired and prayed for victory too, not just out of *national duty*, but secretly for the forbidden, selfish reason that he might come home quickly and safely, her husband, who had promised her the *Roman delights*,

to the little park by the bridge, where old men sat on benches and allowed a little January sun onto their faces after lunch, she felt eyes looking at her belly, her nose and mouth, her figure, she felt protected by her belly and the coat and hat, and yet uncomfortable, it was as if those looks were whips, so she quickened her pace and made straight for the bridge and towards the obelisks, which she could see through the boughs of the trees, of the Piazza del Popolo below the Pincio,

how lucky that you are not blonde, she thought, otherwise they would whistle and make comments, perhaps they see the foreigner in you, *Germans walk differently, Germans hold themselves more stiffly, Italians swing their hips more when they walk, although they actually walk more slowly and languidly, this Roman languidness everywhere, Germans dress more sloppily in civilian clothes and are more proper in uniform, one can recognize a German even before they open their mouth*, said Frau Bruhns, who had been living in Rome for years, on their recent trip to Ostia Antica, perhaps these men notice you because they recognize you as a German, as an Aryan, and because they are not fond of us, do not like their allies in spite of everything the two leaders have sworn, every German in Rome will tell you that, or they can see that you are still a little anxious when you dare to wander around the city alone, without a companion, without the language, without any knowledge, into the sea of the foreign city and foreign people, and perhaps they are making fun of you

really, it does not matter what people think, you have to follow your path, towards the Lungotevere and over the river, and know where you belong, none of these thoughts would bother you in the slightest if you had your husband and protector beside you,

looking left and right, watching out for vehicles which flew past the junction on the Lungotevere at dangerous speeds, as they did everywhere here, the only ones still on the roads belonged to the military or were public service vehicles, and they did not want to be held up by pedestrians, she let pass a slow bus and three cyclists who were struggling on the uneven road surface,

before she reached the bridge which bore her name, as Gert had said, Ponte Margherita, the woman had been a queen, and she had not forgotten that fact, you do not forget queens, particularly if they share your name, and if your own husband

22

lovingly equates you with a queen, high above the famous Tiber,

that sluggish, greeny-grey, greeny-yellow river with a row of houseboats and jetties for swimmers, inanimate and closed off in these winter days, the calm, almost static water reflected the bright, high walls of the riverbanks and the boughs of the trees with single, filthy-brown leaves, beside it well-camouflaged dirty-white and grey-spotted cats sat or lay on the stone banks,

she slowed her pace, looked upstream across the extravagantly wide bridge with waist-high bulbous columns, and thought the view was pretty, she had occasionally crossed the Elbe, the Weser and the Spree, but she had never seen such a majestic river, framed by such fine, bright walls, and which divided the city and yet kept it together too,

she looked downstream to the next bend and the next bridge, just beyond which one might catch sight of the Ponte Sant'Angelo, and found the view even more beautiful, because in this direction you could see, behind the bare trees on the Lungotevere, the *palazzi* in orange, red and ochre plaster, vaunting their towers, terraces and wide balconies,

and in the middle of the Tiber, she was once again struck with astonishment that she of all people was permitted to live in this world city, *in this city of all cities*, as Frau Bruhns said, *she*, who had not even learnt Latin, just about knew the names Romulus and Remus, Caesar and Augustus, understood nothing about art, or about the popes, *she*,

the country girl from Mecklenburg, who like her elder sister had not had any secondary education, the child from the Baltic coast who knew her way around Rostock and Doberan and Eisenach, but was already entirely overwhelmed and out of place in Berlin, *she*, who had only just turned twenty-one, *she* on the Mediterranean and in the most important and magnificent city in Europe, *the navel of the world*, as Gert said, who had shown her the navel of the world at the Forum,

for two months *she* had crossed the Tiber almost every day via the Ponte Margherita, as if that were totally normal, but nothing was totally normal, especially not in these times, each day was a gift, each of the child's movements in her belly a gift, each verse from the Bible and each glance across the Tiber, and so she told herself again,

just how lucky she was, compared to others, compared to him, her beloved husband, who was needed in North Africa, in Tunis, in the desert close to the enemy, instead of in Rome, where he was also needed and urgently awaited, not just by her, and compared to her two younger brothers, who were also now in uniform, or her father in the admiralty in Kiel, or compared to her mother and three sisters in those ever more frequent, terrible nights when sirens wailed, with injuries, deaths, ruins, fires,

no bombs would fall on Rome, that was certain, it was obvious, the English would not raze the Eternal City and the centre of Christendom to the ground, neither would the Americans, and the splendid matt-red *palazzi* from the turn of the century, which she passed on her way to the Piazza del Popolo, their windows adorned with arches, their grand balconies and elegant decorative stonework, were not in imminent danger of collapse, if you could trust those people who were well informed about the war and were confident in their opinions,

she could not join in the discussion, she did not want to join in, she stuck to the belief that she was in the gracious hands of God, that was the one thing that remained certain, the one thing she took for granted,

the view of the brick wall in front of the Piazza and the reverse side of the statue of some sea god which towered high above the wall, a powerful male figure flanked by two half-man, half-fish forms, even from behind the almost naked men presented a strange picture, and the one in the middle carried a sort of huge fork, and when she had walked along here with Gert she had asked why he had a fork in his hand, and, smiling, he had answered,

that's a trident, that's Neptune, the god of the sea, and he's represented by a trident, but you're right, let's call it a fork, he uses it to spear fish for breakfast and shovel them into his mouth, but perhaps the sea god doesn't eat fish at all, it would be like in the Land of Milk and Honey, perhaps he's not allowed to eat any, I didn't pay attention at school, the gods only fed on nectar and ambrosia and drank wine, I'll have to check on whether Neptune ate fish as well,

that was another thing she admired about him, if there was something he did not know, he immediately had an idea where you could find it out,

on the wall, a few metres to either side of the group of figures, fish stood on their heads, a pair on the right and a pair on the left, fat, grinning contentedly, heads adorned with fins, on plinths, bodies and tail fins stretched upwards, looped and twisted around each other, the bodies in contact, the tailfins not touching, but playing with each other in the air, waving over the bodies and heads with acrobatic ease, and the whole thing hewn in stone, *fish in love*, Gert had said, *that's what fish look like when they're in love,* and here, beyond these figures and the fish, Via Ferdinando di Savoia divided, passers-by had to decide whether they wanted to walk left or right along the medium-height wall, past the left- or right-hand pair of lovestruck fish to the Piazza del Popolo, on the gate side or the city side of the magnificent, spacious square, cars and bicycles were directed right into the narrow, one-way street that sloped gently downwards

along which the pedestrian herself mostly walked whenever she went to enquire after letters from her husband or to deliver post at the Wehrmacht headquarters in Via delle Quattro Fontane, the best route to which was by way of Via del Babuino,

but now she chose the left fork, as always when she was on her way to the Pincio and to the church, on the black-grey, greasy paving towards the gate side of the square,

and no matter from which direction she approached, each look, each step was drawn to the massively high obelisk in the centre, a magnet, bordered by four fountains, past which the occasional car drove at a respectable distance,

it was hard to resist this magnet and to avoid walking closer until you were almost at the stepped fountains, upon which stone lions spewed water from their mouths, the same, powerful spurt for centuries, probably, in peacetime and wartime, she stopped, she did not wish to go any closer and make a detour, she came past here almost every day, and yet she stopped each time, to direct her gaze up at the viewing terrace supported by pillars, and the palms and pines of the Pincio, and then slowly let it fall back down to the bright oval square, and wander around and

focus on the shadows of the three large streets which led to the narrow, sombre jungle of the city centre, and then on to the café on the corner until her gaze alighted on the group of sea gods with the fork and the fish lovers, posing above a semi-circular fountain, at the foot of which three cars were parked,

and each time her eyes would then wander up to the tip of the obelisk, to the cross right at the top, she liked this, and found it comforting that the Christian symbol triumphed over the heathen one, according to the Baedeker guide the Egyptian stone was supposed to be three thousand years old,

could you imagine that, older than Christ, perhaps even older than Moses, now a roundabout circled by the odd tiny car and cyclists in black shirts, this incomprehensible limitlessness made her feel dizzy, the very thought of all those things she would never learn or understand made her feel dizzy,

even the Italian that was spoken around her was as alien as the hieroglyphics on the obelisk, and the Latin inscription on the plinth that Gert had translated for her was, apart from the word CAESAR, as unintelligible as the Egyptian characters, the whole of Rome was full of hieroglyphics and puzzles that bewildered her

like the threshing of the corn at the foot of the obelisk in the middle of the piazza that Ilse had talked about, in summer Mussolini always had lorries deliver crops on the Piazza del Popolo, which were then thrown into a threshing machine, bales of straw and sacks of corn were supposed to demonstrate the connection between the countryside and the city, what a waste, and so she was relieved that at least she understood the cross in this square and could abide by the cross and the churches, even if they were Catholic,

and once again, before she continued on her way, she looked to the left of the twin churches into Via del Babuino, down which she had already walked four times this week, Monday and Tuesday, Thursday and Friday, the street of letters and packages, the street of the signs of life she hoped for, the street of happiness, from where she had returned yesterday with two letters from Gert, received at the Wehrmacht headquarters, full of gratitude after a first glance at his lines and the silent, short prayer: *He's alive! Thank you, O benevolent God!*, and this is why, of the three streets which ran radially between the domed churches towards the obelisk, she knew Babuino best of all, her street of happiness and gratitude,

in the first few weeks she often had made part of the journey to Via delle Quattro Fontane by bus, until one day a man, a total stranger, a man of about fifty in a good suit, had touched her bottom, had touched *her*, the manifestly pregnant young lady, with his groping hand, with an unbelievable nerve, the like of which she had never experienced before,

it thus took her too long to react and scream, which she failed to do because, as she was about to scream, she started to feel ashamed that her body had been defiled, and immediately thought that, as a foreigner, as a suspicious German without the language, she would have been just as unable to explain her screaming to the other people as she would have this brute's behaviour, so instead of screaming loudly she had turned and pushed her way to the door, to get out at the next stop,

a distressing moment, and on Via del Corso too, which she had avoided since, the main street with the upmarket shops, almost cleared out by the war, and a memorial plaque for Goethe, who was called Volfango here, the most distressing moment of her nine weeks in Rome, which she had not told any of the deaconesses about, not even Ilse, she had only confided in Gert, who tried to comfort her from Africa, *that's very rich*, he had written, *particularly given your condition*, unfortunately such sick men did exist, and this sort of thing happened more often in Catholic countries, he had written, but she had been right to get off the bus straight away,

since that incident she had kept as far away from crowds as possible, out of consideration for the child as well, and in the dangerous sea of the hospitable and harsh, beautiful and uncanny city, had sought out her little islands of reassurance, such as crosses on obelisks or the church of Santa Maria del Popolo, along the side façade of which she now walked towards the Pincio steps, the only one of the over-elaborate, proudly grandiose churches in which she did not feel alienated,

because Martin Luther had once stayed in the convent here, and said Mass in front of the altar and preached, when he was a young monk in Rome, as she knew from Gert, appalled and disgusted by the improvident extravagance, lack of belief and licentiousness of senior as well as junior church dignitaries, *you could say that here*, Gert had told her, *in this corner of Rome, the seed of the Reformation was sown,*

and then he had shown her a painting, the conversion of Paul, a blinded Paul hurled to the ground by the impact of the conversion and lying under his horse, and Gert had said that it was almost a Protestant painting, its conception inspired so radically by faith, she had forgotten the name of the painter,

each time she felt good when she passed this church on the way to her church, and felt a warmth that emanated from the perceived closeness of Luther and the converted Paul and from the gentle afternoon sun, and she stepped past the sphinxes sitting on the wall of the square up to the Pincio steps, had to dodge a cyclist in a blue skirt with a conspicuously blithe, even happy expression on her face, who shot down the street, and she saw the exertion of the climb that awaited her, seventy or eighty shallow steps that curved gently to the left to a point halfway up the hill,

Dr Roberto's funny phrases in her head, *yes, the steps are good too, walk if you like to walk, until the birth you walk as much you want, young lady, healthy lady, no problem at all, just straining not good, walking better than in bus driving into hole in road*, and better than cycling, she was looking forward to that as well after her pregnancy, to get on a bicycle again and relish dashing downhill, as happy as that young woman,

and she caught her breath before she started shifting her heavy body step by step upwards, on the right-hand side, where the light stone steps had been worn down, something she had only seen on old wooden staircases, and halfway up she turned round again, taking a short rest,

and whispered to her child, who seemed to enjoy being carried upwards and rocked, soon you'll see this too, the beautiful oval of this broad, light square, and the sea god with his fork and everything here, and then she continued upwards, carefully because the stones were greasy and slippery, it was not only when it was wet that you had to walk especially slowly and carefully, it was also important to take care now, and be deliberate with each step,

two German soldiers in uniform approached her, one slipped with the smooth soles of his boots, almost fell onto the steps but recovered and shouted *Scheisse!*, which startled her, because it was not something you said, not as a soldier and role model, and especially not in public right beside Luther's church, as a German in your ally's country you had to behave properly, and she tried her best to avoid being recognized by these two and other passers-by as a German, she wanted nothing to do with men who said *Scheisse!*,

and climbed the last few steps, panted lightly, relieved to have completed the most strenuous part of today's journey, she briefly thought about whether she should now continue upwards via the narrow Pincio road or the steeper, winding footpath, where a black cat darted out of the bushes, pursued by a larger, mangy-looking feline, and decided to begin by turning left, past the closed door to the convent, clearly no longer used, where Luther once stayed, to the stone basin perched on a pedestal,

Gert and she, as if one and the same person, had both said bathtub when they spotted it during their one and only walk together through Rome nine weeks ago, one could imagine that at some point during these two and a half thousand years, it would have been commonplace for the Romans with their loose morals to take a bath in the open air, after all there were several more of these around, such as the two large bathtub fountains on the square in front of the Palazzo Farnese, a building she especially liked because it was one of the few names she could keep in her head, it was also the name of her street,

and behind the stone basin, which was on a platform high up on the ancient Roman city wall, there was the view of the roofed entrance gate to the Villa Borghese and the stone eagles and griffins which kept watch on the crests, sculptures of eagles and griffins were to be found everywhere in the park, they must be heraldic beasts,

once she had become aware of the fact she started to discover one eagle after the other, on buildings, statues, plinths, fountains, bridges, and she was surprised because she had always thought of the eagle as a German heraldic beast, as a German peculiarity, and initially she had thoroughly disapproved of the fact that it cropped up so regularly in Italy,

something fascinated her from the start about these eagles, they looked familiar and yet different, it had taken her a while to solve the puzzle and identify the difference, the German eagles looked sterner, they stood erect down to the last feather, fanned their wings in military fashion, or clutched the swastika,

whereas the Italian eagles were represented more like real eagles, almost like pets, with softer, more naturally formed feathers, stern also, but watching and waiting, they were more paternally strict and protective than militarily correct, and she had to admit that she preferred the Italian eagles, particularly these four, flanked by grinning, smirking griffins which, at her eye-level, looked out in every direction from the roof of the entrance gate to the Villa Borghese,

she had always wanted to ask Gert why there were so many eagles in Rome, it must have something to do with the ancient Romans, with Caesar, Augustus, Romulus, everything was somehow connected with the ancient Romans, he would, no doubt, have been able to tell her off the top of his head, it seemed that he had an answer to all her questions, but there was so much to write every day, so much she had to tell him, so many worries of his to dispel, to convey comfort in confident handwriting, hope and trust in God in exemplary German handwriting, and place her love in every sentence, because each letter might be the last, she would have found it completely ridiculous, even disturbing if the question of the eagles' origin had become a main topic of her letters to Africa,

and, her thoughts focused on the letter she was going to write to him that evening, she carried on, past a life-size, smiling lion made from that white marble-like stone which could be seen everywhere here, and whose name she had forgotten, on beyond the bend in the road, and slowly along the path marked with shallow steps and lined with laurel bushes and gnarled trees, and as ever

when she became melancholic at the thought of her lover redeployed to the front, she comforted herself with the phrase that was his phrase too, *better than being an infantryman in Russia*, the last few steps stood before her, she looked straight ahead at the shallow steps, a pace apart, Africa is better than Russia, desert better than snow, one step, orderly room better than infantry, another step, lance corporal better than corporal, another step, he was alive, many had died or gone missing, yet another step, and he could look forward to the child with her, and one more, and he was close, just beyond the sea, far away and close at the same time, very close,

when she thought of Ilse's fiancé, who was stuck in Australia, interned by the British, how fortunate she was compared to Ilse, who while waiting in Rome for her final papers for the boat journey to see her fiancé in Australia was surprised by the outbreak of war, and since that time, now more than three years ago, had been working uncomplainingly as a housemaid for the deaconesses, and was longing for the end of the war,

grateful for her unwarranted good fortune and slightly out of breath, she thus reached the magnificent top of the Pincio, the place of her most painful sorrow, up here on the day after her arrival, finally approved by the authorities, on 11th November, at the end of a long, day-long walk, the first and only walk they had taken together through the city of wonders, Gert had told her with many oaths of love, as he stammered and fought back the tears, what a note from the Wehrmacht the previous day had said, the day of her arrival from Germany:

Order for deployment! Africa! Day after tomorrow!, up here on the broad viewing terrace, on the square named after the wild warrior Napoleon, with the most beautiful view in the world, the Baedeker guide claimed, over roofs, hills and sky, was where she had been dumbstruck by the order,

a shock which paralyzed her limbs, extinguished the promised delights, she had sobbed in the arms of her husband, united yesterday, separated the day after tomorrow, three days, it was incomprehensible, she was unable to stop crying in spite of his kisses, all those lovely plans shattered, an incomprehensible, overwhelming disappointment,

while in the background horns had sounded and bells chimed on the children's carousel, and the croaky, laughing voice of the entertainer from the puppet theatre had provided a commentary to the whole thing as if in mockery, just as now, as she recalled that dreadful moment, the carousel rang out and the puppeteer crowed once more,

for in spite of her parents' opposition she had departed from Mecklenburg with a hard-earned visa for the unimaginably far-off Italy, to the friendly and alien country, to the dangerous, unsafe, Catholic Rome, to the father of her child, after he had been recalled by the Wehrmacht to carry out light duties in Rome because of an injury and a tissue inflammation which would not heal, and so he was discharged for his real work, that of strengthening people's faith in God, and the two of them had imagined that they would finally be together, together for the first time since their wedding, not yet together in an apartment, but with a little attic room for her in Via Alessandro Farnese, with the midwives' ward three floors below, and a room for him in Via Toscana next to the church, together at last and only separated by a good half-hour's walk, the last three months of her pregnancy, and then together again in the city safe from bombs, ready for the *Roman delights*, as Gert was fond of saying,

all of this conceived in vain, in vain the battle with her parents won, in vain the papers for her visa and the forms filled out and stamped for foreign currency, in vain the months of planning and the twenty-four hours of travelling, she had thought at first,

but then she had to learn again that no suffering is in vain, and she had made good use of this phrase to console herself over the past few weeks, she had not, in spite of her mother's desperate pleas, returned home to the Reich, for in Rome she was closer to him, a reunion was far more likely here than in Germany, than in the small Mecklenburg town of Doberan, the trial both of them had to endure was easier to suffer in Rome, she thought again,

as right on the parapet of the viewing platform, beside a group of close-cropped Italian children in uniform, boys in shorts about seven or eight years old, she looked down at the Piazza del Popolo and the now tiny sea god with his fork, at the long shadow of the obelisk and the endless landscape of roofs and domes, none of which she could name except for the dome of St Peter's which dominated all else,

certainly she would have been better able to recall all these churches and *palazzi* with their unfamiliar names if the Wehrmacht had kept its promise and spared him, rather than giving the order for *redeployment*, and if her husband had stayed beside her, her husband who, ever since that shock in the evening sun on the Pincio, had consoled her time and again that this was not some horrible blind chance at play, and had strengthened her belief that *God, who is love, delivers this all to us, that it may benefit us in the end*,

for it was un-Christian to shed tears for one's own misfortune and to forget the far greater misfortunes of others, the joys of life were limitless, every day she could delight in her child, and today she might look forward to the church concert and the cantatas, she heard Gert say,

life is like a Bach cantata, the first thing we hear is that we can be helped, then we may lament, then we hear the Bible's answer, then we may doubt, look inside ourselves and pray, then we hear Jesus speak, and at the end we find ourselves in the redemptive choir amongst the triumphant trumpets,

and in wartime, life was a very particular sort of trial, God's most difficult trial, in spite of all the tears your individual plans counted for nothing, the selfish hope of the *Roman delights* counted for nothing, all human endeavour counted for nothing, *for my thoughts are not your thoughts, says the Lord,*

she said silently to herself, looking at the cross on top of the obelisk, the sphinx figures on the walls which surrounded the square, the busy streets beyond, the bridge named Margherita, she could almost see the entire route she had come along, and she listened to the teacher

talk about the city to the children who, in spite of their uniform, were not particularly disciplined, one of them, snotty-nosed and with chilblains on his legs, began to imitate the Duce, followed by three of his classmates, then they gave the Hitler salute, the Roman salute from the Pincio balcony to an imaginary crowd on the square below,

which the teacher immediately forbade them from doing before continuing her talk, while the young woman could not understand a word except for *via*, *piazza* and *obelisco*, she could not even make out the names of the streets and hills from the hasty melody of this language, yet she did not feel alien, at least not up here on the Pincio, where the heavens were close, not even in St Peter's Basilica or the Pantheon could you get closer to the heavens, and with the view, now familiar to her, to the south over the city lit up by the mild January sun, as far as the royal palace set up high, and the huge, blinding-white marble cake of the so-called Altar of the Fatherland,

bothered only by the coy or cheeky glances the boys gave her swollen belly, some sniggered as if they had never seen their mothers, aunts, or neighbours highly pregnant, but perhaps the objectionable thing about it, the thing she noticed, was that she had been once again recognized as a foreigner, a pregnant foreigner, even the adults here thought that was not right somehow,

she moved away from the children's intrusive glances and sniggers, and walked across the gravel towards the stalls and the puppet theatre, and now the changing voices of the puppeteer rang more loudly in her ears, from a distance she could see the figures bash each other, fall down, stand up again, and, making her way resolutely towards her goal, she turned to the path beneath the trees and thought about her husband, thought about why he had chosen this place on the Pincio that late afternoon to mention the terrible order, and she was grateful to him that he had been wise enough not to disclose to her immediately upon her arrival at the station the evening before, nor that morning, the order he could do nothing about, wise enough to show her first the columns, façades, streets, ruins, views of the city, embed in her all those beautiful and new things, and plant the images in her mind, so far as it was possible in one day, unclouded by the shadow of a terrible disappointment, wise enough to take her, on a late sunny afternoon, up to the Pincio and introduce her to this most beautiful of all views,

before telling her, like a confession, the dreadful truth of the *immediate redeployment*, giving her comforting kisses, then pointing to the royal palace and the shining block of marble of the Altar of the Fatherland and saying,

that's south, that's south-west, and from up here you have the best view towards Africa, beyond those hills you can see from here, beyond the Tiber valley over there on the left is the coast, beyond that the sea, and on the other side of the sea, in the south, there I'll be standing and I'll see you up here on the Pincio, and you'll see me over there in Africa, and we'll wave to each other every evening, and send each other a kiss from coast to coast,

he had repeated the play on words with coast and kiss until both of them started laughing, a brief laugh between sobs, and he told her that kissing in public was frowned upon in Italy, lovers and fiancés were almost liable to be punished if they kissed or embraced in the park, and married couples automatically refrained from doing so, the Fascists wanted to be exceptionally decent people, and they did not tolerate anything as indecent as kisses or laughter,

she longed for such kisses and moments of laughter, which would make even the tears and pain of that November evening acceptable, and she was certain that she had not laughed since,

she turned around once more to the spot where all this had taken place, other couples were now looking down on the square, hesitantly keeping their distance from each other, the schoolchildren jostled in front of the puppet theatre, no doubt having already forgotten the pregnant foreigner,

while she wondered whether in a few years' time her child, if it were to be a boy, would snigger as rudely as these schoolboys in the presence of a pregnant woman, the child did not move, gave no answer with its arms or legs, she just felt confident that with the correct upbringing all would be fine, *even the trivial things are important*, Gert had written, and as she promised herself that she would be as good a mother as her own mother had been,

she continued her way under the trees whose names she did not know, and each time this troubled her, for in Germany she could identify every tree, often from a distance, down to the yews and ashes, she had been the best in her League of German Girls group, at flower identification too, but here in Italy she had not yet got beyond palms, cypresses, ilexes and pines,

her way between the stone busts on tall plinths of famous Italians, the entire park, including the side paths and the areas around the small obelisks, was littered with these bright stone heads, all of them men whose names meant nothing to her, Ratazzi or Rossi or Secchi, some faces washed away by the weather, others still with sharp profiles, sixty, eighty, perhaps more than a hundred heads, and she could not help thinking

that so many die each day on the battle-fronts, each head a life, each life a gift, each life at the centre of other lives, although she knew that every day it was thousands more than these men here, but with these heads, all so different from each other, it was easier to imagine what each individual life meant, just how many hopes, efforts, joys and pains, and yet she felt how narrow her power of imagination was, because in truth she was only thinking of one life, the one which influenced and affected her most,

in passing she saw an old woman sitting alone on a bench between the many stone heads, singing to herself, now louder, now softer, giving the impression of being mentally ill or perhaps just deeply troubled, with a croaky voice, a warning to beware, you must not go mad amongst all these stone heads, amongst too many dead bodies,

and she turned away with a glance to the left, where two German officers got out of a car outside a splendid villa and walked up the steps to the entrance, she had often seen military men go into this building or, on sunny days during these winter weeks, sit on the terraces in their long coats, German and Italian officers, who met to make decisions about the war's progress and who could drink coffee here in the luxury of their own positions of responsibility,

probably the good, genuine coffee like the one Gert occasionally sent her from Tunis, and which Roman housewives had not been able to buy for a long time, or only on the black market at unbelievable prices,

she was quite happy her husband was not an officer, that he was even proud of the fact he was still just a lance corporal, an orderly, a driver, a clerk and telephonist, and that instead of planning great battles, making decisions about the life and death of thousands, and slurping coffee in luxury, he was happier giving her the advice to become better acquainted with art and, here in the park, to go further on to the left, to stroll to the other end as far as the Galleria Borghese, *go there, have a look around, enjoy the beautiful things,* but she was afraid of getting to know art on her own, and she was also uneasy about the nakedness that was on display and painted there, which Ilse had told her about, and she could not tell Raphael apart from Michelangelo, although she had seen the Michelangelo film with Gert in Berlin, Sistine Chapel, Moses, sure, but what was it about pictures,

each time she visited a museum, as she had again recently with the cultured Frau Bruhns on the Capitol, she realized how much she relied on having her husband beside her, by herself she could not get excited, only with his eyes and explanations would she have been able to feel happiness, understand better what she was looking at, you can only see properly when you are together, only when you are together does the meaning reveal itself,

and she looked from the Viale del Belvedere, which continued along the top of the hill in the direction of the Spanish Steps to the church of the Trinità dei Monti, towards the south in the direction of Africa, she fixed her gaze between the royal palace and the Altar of the Fatherland into the distance as far as Tunis,

where he sat in a captain's study on the edge of the city from six or seven in the morning until midnight, he was not allowed to be more specific about his military work or reveal where it was, even the place names in his letters were kept as general as possible, *Africa, 7th January*, and only once, it might have been an oversight or perhaps a clue for her, he had written Tunis instead of Africa,

in the meantime she had learnt that the battle lost at the end of October in the desert at El Alamein had been the reason for the surprise relocation order in November, for the shock of their separation, tens of thousands of soldiers had died, Germans and Italians, this is why they had called up the reservists as quickly as possible, even those in reserved occupations, they had also ordered her husband back to the front, there were to be no more disasters, no more defeats,

Victory! had become an imperative for the Germans, and also for the Italians whose eyes were assaulted every day on large squares, at the corners of broad streets and in the headlines of the wall-newspapers by the bold-type words *Vinceremo!* or *Vincere!*, always with exclamation marks, sometimes with three exclamation marks,

and yet there were too many defeats, in Russia the picture was no longer one of great victories, they hardly spoke about victories any more, they only spoke of the length of the war, and what was the point of this dreadful war if there were to be no more victories, they could not imagine a war without victories, since she was twelve years old the Führer of the German Reich had proceeded from one triumph to the next, for as long as she could remember he had only won, conquered, been celebrated, cheered, even during church services thanks were offered up for the political and military successes too, and her husband would only be able to return soon if they were victorious, but if more defeats threatened on almost all fronts he would stay there, his life in ever-increasing danger, and she would have to wait longer and longer,

it was impossible to think what might become of the beautiful Germany without victories, thinking this was forbidden, she forbade herself from thinking it, and while her yearning flew south to Africa,

Wartburg castle appeared before her eyes, as if the hills and valleys of Rome were similar to the hills and valleys of the Thuringian Forest around the Wartburg, and the Roman roofs similar to the Thuringian treetops, and the villas on the Gianicolo similar to the villas of Eisenach, nothing was comparable, and yet the proud, beautiful German Wartburg with its towers and gates, battlements, the walls and rows of windows of the long buildings were all of a sudden quite close, the destination of their first walk together, when their love began to germinate two and a quarter years ago, instead of going to Café Tigges the young man, who she had made wait two years before agreeing to a date, had suggested a stroll up to the Wartburg, their first hour of getting to know each other a walk up through larches, oaks and beeches, their timid, solemn steps together on the castle's land, made sacred by Luther, and the view into the distance from the south tower, formal conversations about her education and his time in the army and about her family and his family on the path to the Sängerwiese park and while drinking a coffee outside,

in beautiful October weather, it was the first time she had dared to go for a walk alone with a young man, back down from the Wartburg through the Marienthal, and at the end of this long day his question as to whether he might come again, from Kassel to Eisenach, and see her once more, before he travelled to Rome,

yes, she had said, but so softly that he had to ask her again, *yes*, she had repeated a little louder, and blushed, blushed like never before, and a few days later,

he was back with chocolates that he had bought in France, where he had been a soldier, bought, not taken, he had emphasized, they strolled through the woods below the Wartburg and ate the chocolates, and in the evening he took her by surprise with the cautious question of whether he might already address her using the informal *du*, because the formal *Sie* was so ghastly, and after the first *du* everything had gone at the speed of light until their engagement,

for this reason she was not at all surprised to see the Wartburg on the Roman horizon like a Fata Morgana, the impregnable fortress, towering high above the woods, was a symbol for the belief that He, the God written with a capital H, would, with the verse from the Bible, *He leadeth me in the paths of righteousness*, help her and had helped her to react correctly to the letter from her suitor,

and at the same time was a symbol for the belief in their love, which had been awakened in the October sun below this castle, and had grown to become the gift of an immeasurable happiness, the first words of love etched in her memory, *I think you are far too good for me, and I fear I do not have enough to give you*,

each one of these syllables, against which at first she had protested in vain, *you think far too well of me*, and all his declarations of love that followed she had written down before the wedding and she bore them in her heart, they gave her strength in every moment of anxiety and helped in her Roman solitude, and here too, on the Pincio path,

where she walked along the high walls of the Villa Medici and looked over to the dome of St Peter's, faith and love belonged together, they were inseparable, without her faith in God's providence she would not have been able to accept this love and

a man who had only seen her once, before she had even turned seventeen, at an *aesthetic evening* for young people with singing, games and dancing, and although he had not been her dinner partner had danced with her and, soon afterwards, sent a letter asking whether he might meet her, while she, because she had not been able to recall his name, did not even know which of the young men had written to her, and had declined to enter into a correspondence, *because I feel too young and have only just turned seventeen years old, such a correspondence is always a slight commitment, and I should like to be completely free in this respect*,

a man who had waited two years for her, from autumn 1938 through the start of the war and the French campaign up to autumn 1940, and had then written, *of all the experiences in my life I have not forgotten that evening when I got to know you only briefly, it amazes me, but I really wanted to write to tell you that the thought of you has not left me since*,

and after this unbelievable letter had reached her in Eisenach via three offices she replied, enraptured by the patience and persistence of this stranger, with a postcard and then they arranged the meeting in the café that led to the first Wartburg walk, which was followed by a second, and their engagement less than a fortnight later,

because she, as befits a good daughter, had sent a short letter to her mother after the first meeting, and a longer one after the second meeting, and at the same time had told everything to the head of the kindergarten teacher-training college, Tante Emma von Rentorff, who had asked the man to come and see her, gained a very favourable impression of him, and relayed this by telephone to Bad Doberan and, as there were only a few days left before he departed for Rome on church duties,

to Via Sicilia, along which she now walked, pregnant, and, her thoughts drifting back to the sequence of events, still astonished and overcome with gratitude for all those fortunate acts of providence,

her parents demanded not only that this young man should present himself to them, but also that the engagement should take place immediately, having found the favourable impression of their barely nineteen-year-old daughter's suitor confirmed, which unsettled him greatly as he was not used to such pious customs, after only twelve days and three meetings with his future bride, before he had to yield to these wishes after a long conversation with her, and then at the edge of the woods, near Heiligendamm, sealed with a kiss something that had begun in the shade of the Wartburg's trees and was to become a *life's journey* as in the poem

I have made my way to you through life, / as unmistakably as the dove, / although so long in captivity, / soared over green fields to find her way home, this is what Börries von Münchhausen had written, these lines contained the complete truth, and it had been the revered and clever Tante Emma who right at the start had advised her to meet the young stranger, *after two years!*, and who had given the two of them the poem after their engagement, *And when I think of storm and strife and striving, / of my youth here and there, / I often feel: My whole life has been / a silent, unwavering passage towards you*,

on her silent, unwavering passages through Rome, the Wartburg was often in her mind, as a symbol of the reliability of love and faith, and of beautiful Germany, but also as a Protestant foil for St Peter's Basilica, Luther's fortress, Luther's strength, Luther's invincibility, Luther's beautiful language, and as a reminder of the clemency and humility of the holy, or rather evangelical paragon Elisabeth, who rebelled against court life and voluntarily lived a life of poverty, helping sick people and children, which is why she became a role model for the young kindergarten teachers trained in Eisenach, she liked to walk through the capital of the Catholic Church with the image of the Wartburg before her, south along the wall of the Villa Medici, on the right-hand side of the street that sloped gently downwards, each step bringing her closer to Africa, looking to the right at the roof gardens and thinking of the wonderful roof garden at the deaconesses' mission and of the benefits that Rome brought,

the fresh fruit on her plate mornings and evenings, something one could only dream of in the Reich, an orange and an apple every day, there had even been grapes in November, fat, blue, sweet grapes, and whenever she had the craving for the greatest luxury, chocolate, she was allowed to go to Gert's room in Via Toscana, to the *sweet drawer*,

also the mild autumn-spring sun on the roof terrace, a room, at first one to herself, now one she shared with Ilse, soon, after the birth, her own one again, even without her beloved husband these were sufficient *Roman delights*, a roof over her head with Christian people and enough to eat, looked after, spoilt, and the sun to boot,

occasionally Gert sent her dates and date paste, raisins, figs and sugar, sometimes almonds, pasta, rice, and fairly regularly, thank goodness, the popular green coffee from Africa in field-post packets that could weigh a maximum of one hundred grams, or once he gave a friend who was travelling to Rome on duty a whole kilo of coffee to take, he received his pay in French currency and almost every week sent one of these tiny packages, either to relatives, or to her, and his friend Jacobi, at the Rome headquarters in Via delle Quattro Fontane, knew a thing or two about dealing and sold the precious goods for her,

or she put it away in the cupboard for a future emergency, coffee kept its value, or for celebrations such as his return from the front or the christening, the coffee was keenly sought on the black market, it had been rationed for years and become even scarcer recently, there was no coffee left in Rome, it fetched unbelievable prices, she was astonished by how valuable coffee was to the Romans, people drank only a substitute coffee and had no more than three slices of bread, how could it go on like that,

Ilse had been born in Brazil, could speak Portuguese, and during her three-year wait had learnt very good Italian, and in her uninhibited manner enjoyed talking to the kitchen and laundry staff, Ilse knew about the Romans' discontent, *the people don't want the war any more*, Ilse had said, *and particularly not when coffee and bread, flour and sugar are taken away from them, and the gas is turned off for hours on end,* these were bold words, you would not have been able to say such things out loud in the Reich, that would have been undermining military morale, and here too, you had to watch out, hopefully Ilse only said these things in their room, when it was just the two of them, Ilse confided in her, but it made her feel uneasy, she was not used to such boldness, that is why she tried just to nod when Ilse talked, at most uttered a soft yes, and otherwise said nothing more,

she did not want to risk getting into trouble and neither did she want to harm the war morale, because what would happen if the Italians no longer wished to fight, or if the war suddenly came to an end, an end without victory, an end without defeat, she could not imagine in the slightest what would become of Germany, of poor Germany, surrounded by enemies,

the war was a difficult trial, and the completely unimaginable period following the war would be a difficult trial too, perhaps even more difficult, that is what the Job story taught, but it was pointless, it was conceited to start thinking about that now, for there was only a single helpful thought, *we are all in the hands of God, and God will make everything right again according to His will and not our will,*

as she approached the fountain with the conspicuously large trough beneath the trees

opposite the Villa Medici, a place which invited you
to stop briefly because the view from here opened
up again, down to the shimmering surfaces of the
city and the dome of St Peter's in the background,

in front of this fountain with a stone ball,
from the apex of which the water flowed, she would
always be reminded of the school poem about
the *Roman Fountain, The stream rises and falls /
to fill the round marble trough*, even though the
description did not match this fountain at all, she
still knew the poem by heart because she loved the
way it ended, *And each one gives and takes alike /
and flows and stills*,

and onwards past a coffee stand from
better times, when there was coffee, when there
were no shortages, she had never seen the man
behind the counter busy with the mighty silver-
and-copper espresso machine crowned by a
bronze eagle, he sometimes gave her a friendly
or ambiguously friendly smile if she did not look
away in time as she passed by, and nobody had ever
sat at the four tables in front of the stand,

as if the espresso machine and the empty
tables were waiting for the end of the war, it would
be a beautiful spot here, opposite the Villa Medici,
in peacetime, sipping beside the fountain that
much-too-strong coffee that the Italians loved,
two old men were standing by the counter, talking
to the barman, she looked away sharply, did not

want to be met by suggestive glances, and focused straight ahead at the towers and flank of the Trinità dei Monti with the obelisk in front,

and because Ilse was likeable in spite of her outspoken manner, because her circumstances were especially difficult and she knew so much about Rome, for example she knew why children ran around with snotty noses, their parents did not have the money to buy handkerchiefs, and most people did not have heating in winter and wore coats to bed, hence the chilblains,

she worried about Ilse, who rarely had a good word to say about authority that was invested by God, about Hitler and Mussolini, only a few days ago she had said Hitler always demanded that people *show no weakness*, but human beings were not made like that, and Mussolini always demanded that people *had to hate the enemy*, but the Italians that she knew were not fond of hatred, why should they hate the English and Americans,

fortunately Ilse had broken off at this point, perhaps out of consideration for her, because she, the younger woman, who was always silent when national and political questions were discussed, had just for a second wondered why it *was* necessary to hate the British and Americans, and in the same instant this forbidden thought made her feel guilty, confused and horrified, because after all they were fighting against her husband, against the Germans and Italians in Africa, and causing so much suffering to innocent people with their bombs that fell on towns and cities, and it was not only houses that were being destroyed, but churches as well, what would the Romans say if their churches were flattened, for example this famous one above the Piazza di Spagna, which she was now approaching, and whose bells were suspended in the semi-open tower, as if they were just about to start ringing,

perhaps, she thought, you ought to keep your distance from Ilse, at the very least stop getting into discussions with her, Ilse is older and more experienced, but clearly faith is not so important to her, she rarely speaks about it and neither does she go to church every Sunday, perhaps that is the reason for her strange opinions, on the other hand one had to feel pity for her and understand her, she had been waiting for more than three years now for this journey to her fiancé in far-off Australia, for that reason alone she must wish that the war were over,

Ilse did not like Rome obsessives either, those who could only see the ancient city or the *palazzi*, altars, columns and works of art, and who quoted Goethe or the fountain poems at every opportunity, because these addicts, according to her, knew nothing of the day-to-day starvation, or of the outer suburbs where people kept chickens and rabbits on balconies, or of the simple people and the dreadful poverty, on which all the splendour was founded,

the people in the laundry, in the laundry press, down below at the heated mangle and in the kitchen, they could sing a very different Roman song from the educated Germans with their eye for superficial beauty, from the academics at the institutes and the German aristocrats at the two embassies, the black embassy at the Vatican and the white one of the King and the Duce,

for example, the Rome obsessives from the upper classes surely had no idea that the Romans had been advised to bake so-called war cakes, without cake flour or butter, but instead using pasta dough, and then to save the water they cooked pasta in and wash themselves with it, it was supposed to be as good as soap, another thing that no longer existed, and how much propaganda there was about cooking water being the best soap, and propaganda about so-called war gardens in squares or on free plots of land in the city itself, such as in front of the Altar of the Fatherland, where they were growing vegetables because these were in very short supply,

she had been struck by the term German aristocrats, even though Ilse was not wrong about this, as a Christian you always had to look to how the poor were faring, and it was true that in Rome, too, most people were poor, the many victories and conquests had not eliminated poverty, but only made things worse, and

what should people abide by if they, as Ilse claimed, were told how they should talk and greet each other, and if they were forced to join the party just to get a portion of fish or half-price cinema tickets,

but even if all that were true and Ilse were not exaggerating, you had to be wary of exaggeration and generalizations, it was still no reason to run down Germans from the educated classes or German aristocrats, who no doubt had a deeper insight into things than Ilse, it was not Christian either to feel superior to others and pass disparaging comments, and after all, even if the surname she had borne for the last year and a half gave no indication, she was a German aristocrat too, albeit without a deeper insight into things,

she felt, in fact, that Germans from the nobility were particularly friendly and helpful towards her, she could do nothing about her background, nor about the fact that she knew no Italians apart from Dr Roberto, who always said, *walk young lady, please don't be making worries, I look after everything, walk!*, and now she had completed that lovely long stretch as far as the Spanish Steps, cared for in the German *colony* and the German community, she could not help the fact that she was more fortunate than the poor Romans, and that she had little more to do than to find baby clothes and knit, write letters, and walk four or five times a week to the Wehrmacht headquarters, from where the field post was collected and sent, and to help the nuns, in the kitchen, with the cleaning, and with the baking and decorations for Christmas,

a Christmas with the nuns almost like that at home, with a tree, lametta and candles, 'Lo, How a Rose E'er Blooming', 'Oh Thou Joyful Day' and 'Silent Night' in Via Alessandro Farnese with the Christmas gospel and white tablecloths, with biscuits and presents, a writing pad, *Hermann und Dorothea*, baby things, with apples, almonds, oranges, figs, nuts, with a long letter from Gert and a package from Bad Doberan, for the first time Christmas far away from her family and yet without any homesickness, while in Tunis, after 'Silent Night' had been sung, Gert had been obliged to endure a tedious evening with the men getting horribly drunk,

now Christmas was over, now there were about four weeks until the birth, and nobody could criticize her for only helping out with light chores in the kitchen, or that there was little more for her to do than wait for her child and her husband, the arrival of her child could be worked out approximately, but the arrival of her husband, who had promised to show her the interiors of the most important churches, including this one, Trinità dei Monti, could not be estimated, it depended on the highest powers, on God's will and how the war progressed, he had left her the Baedeker and advised her to look around, *in Rome there is something beautiful to discover every day*,

and every day she did find something beautiful, such as the view now from the balustrade down the curved, sweeping Spanish Steps, all her friends and relatives back in the Reich would envy her for this view, which was also said to be the most beautiful in Rome and which she was able to enjoy, as if in passing, on the way from her room to the church,

just above the tallest buildings in the city centre with the labyrinth of roofs and roof tiles, chimneys and domes, as well as the winter sun, dipping above St Peter's Basilica, and sharpening the profile of the hills on the horizon and the narrow bands of clouds,

and she could let her eyes wander from the generously wide steps to the palms and the façades in those bright southern colours, and to the roof terraces which housed plants in winter too, and two shining orange and lemon trees behind a bush in a garden on the left, and back up again to the domes and roofs and the first traces of the evening light,

who would not wish to trade places with her, in Rome, above these steps where you could feel the whole of the sky, in the south, in the land of grapes and oranges, and no bombs, to stroll amidst a mild war whose only symptoms were sirens, and then to a concert, and yet,

she was allowed to think this without feeling ungrateful, it was here, especially, that she missed the voice and the knowledge, the warmth and closeness of her husband, who belonged to her, she wished to see Rome as he did, not according to the Baedeker, she would have loved to know how he would react to her comment that, in these famous Spanish Steps of bright, porous limestone, at which people never ceased to marvel, she saw a ladder to heaven, the heavenly ladder of Jacob from the Bible, from the illustrated Bible of her childhood,

a beautifully curved, slightly bent ladder to heaven, which from below, from the city's streets and the terrestrial, from the boat fountain and the shops beyond it, led up via twists, detours, balustrades and platforms affording rest, heavenwards to the obelisk and the church set high up, *And he dreamt, and behold a ladder set up on the earth, and the top of it reached to heaven, and behold the angels of God ascending and descending on it,*

the Baedeker said something about Rococo or Baroque, this meant nothing to her, but the passage from the Bible most certainly did, and she would have loved to know whether here, in the centre of Rome, it was acceptable to think of the father of the Israelites,

given that she was Aryan, after all, and was not allowed to speak about the Jews, even the figures from the Old Testament were somehow suspicious, particularly Jacob who in this passage, she had checked it up, is summoned to make the people of Israel disperse in all directions of the world, and that was precisely the problem with the Jews, who were responsible for the unhealthy mixing of the races, as she had learnt at school and in the League of German Girls,

perhaps there were even Jews in Rome, she did not know, she could not recall having seen any, maybe wearing yellow stars on their coats, and she had not heard the thorny word Jew uttered by any of her Roman acquaintances, not even Ilse,

it could be dangerous if, in passing, you thought of something as simple as the ladder to heaven, even if it was not angels going up and down but normal Romans, city people who bestowed no glances of amazement or pride upon the wonder which they used as a short cut between the upper and lower city, just one old man, selling freshly roasted chestnuts in the middle of the steps, seemed to have something of the reverence and patience of an angel,

at any rate, you could not expect joyful, frisky steps and laughing faces in these times, not even on a ladder to heaven, but perhaps some people striding more respectfully or at least sitting on the steps and enjoying the magnificent view,

she would have been able to discuss the Jews and her Jewish thoughts with Gert, were he here, but not with anybody else, this was another reason she needed him beside her, so she could talk about something so awkward, about the danger of the ideas that came into her head,

on her own she could not work out what you were allowed and not allowed to say, what you should think and what you ought not to think, and how to cope with her ambivalent feelings, all she could do was to keep these things to herself until his return,

once Gert had said, and her father used to say something similar too, when he spoke about Christian principles, *our God, our Bible, our faith are greater than all reason, and also greater than all the figures of authority we include in our intercessionary prayers in church, so that they may act responsibly, but if the Führer places himself above God and God's will, then we must not obey him blindly, and neither does the Bible say that we are against the Jews or must fight against them, our faith is closely connected to their faith, therefore it is wrong to malign them for everything*, this is roughly what the men of the Confessing Church said, who were of similar mind to her father and husband, things that could only be communicated secretly and quietly,

it was all so difficult, GOD WITH US stood on the soldiers' belt buckles, above an eagle on a swastika, God and Führer were united on every uniform, even Gert wore God and the eagle and the swastika across his stomach, but he did not like to talk about it, it was all too difficult,

in any case it was better to keep quiet, and as a woman it was even more important to restrain oneself, how quickly an idea or a thought can escape from one's lips, improvident words could help the enemy, *The enemy is listening!*, she had learnt, or it might be dangerous on a personal level,

there is the weapon of silence and the weapon of words, she had learnt with the League of German Girls, and as she preferred to remain silent anyway, especially if she was not confident of her thoughts and her faint doubts were not assuaged, she knew what she had to do, to trust patiently in God, and continue undeterred along her path, and, as she turned around and cast the obelisk a brief, backwards glance, she noticed a human figure on it, on his knees before a bird-person, which immediately made her wonder

whether they would soon start boarding up this obelisk with its oddities, the Spanish Steps and the lovely boat fountain, or use sand and concrete to protect and clad them because of the ever more frequent air-raid warnings,

as they had the other sights you could no longer see, such as the equestrian statue of an emperor on the Capitol, a large picture of which was in the Baedeker, now enclosed in a shed-like construction with protective timbers, the Arch of Constantine packed on all sides by sandbags, Michelangelo's Moses bricked up, or the tall, ancient Roman columns supported by vast wooden scaffolding,

these protective structures were to be seen ever more frequently in the city centre, sometimes daubed with propaganda such as *Vincere! Vincere! Vinceremo!* or with maps of the Italian Empire including Abyssinia and the North African conquests that in the meantime were being intensely fought over or had already been lost once again,

why did they not also secure the balustrades, steps and railings of the Spanish ladder to heaven or the obelisk with the bird-person from possible bomb attacks as they had the other works as a safety precaution, like the other safety precautions, after all you had to show the population that safety was being attended to, even though no bombs fell on Rome, no bombs would fall on the city of antiquity and of the Pope, in the city with the silly, albeit in wartime useful moniker, Eternal, which the British and Americans knew and respected too,

and which no doubt the German military respected also, three naval officers stepped out of the hotel beside the church, a very posh hotel, so posh that she only dared to glance momentarily at the revolving door and the porter with his blue- and gold-braided uniform, who saw off the officers with a snappy salute, but not the Hitler salute or the Roman salute, which Hitler had borrowed from the Italian Fascists, who in turn had imitated the ancient Romans,

from Via Sistina a horse and cart crossed the officers' path, they stood there, faintly amused, and then strolled across the street to the barrow of a souvenir seller, who was waiting for customers by the steps,

even the Germans, even the military loved Rome, even the Germans would never do anything to harm the splendour of the Eternal City, the capital of their allies the Italians, here every officer saw the Holy Roman Empire of the German Nation from the history books, all Germans that she had met here were agreed on that, especially those within the Church or Church hierarchy, most of whom were not *official people*, as Gert said, but nobody believed that even fervent National Socialists would harm sacrosanct Rome, however bad the war situation,

Augustus, the Pope and Goethe, Frau Bruhns said, *will see to it that Rome remains safe and that we can survive here*, and the somewhat idealistic Herr Bruhns said, *and even if the British couldn't give two figs for our Goethe, those gentlemen will not bomb the graves of Keats and Shelley*, Frau Bruhns may have said Caesar instead of Augustus, she could no longer remember, Herr Bruhns may have cited other English names, she could no longer remember,

she heard phrases like this over and over again, and yet there was a blackout from half-past five in the evening until half-past six in the morning, and she was not thinking about Goethe or the Pope, at this precise moment she was thinking about the strange bird-person on the obelisk, about the two old horses as well, about the chickens and rabbits on the balconies, which she had never seen, and she thought about her child, she prayed to be allowed to bring her child into the world during a night without sirens and without bombs falling on the world, and as she turned now into a dark Via Sistina, between the posh hotel and a splendid corner house, which, like a ship's bow, towered high above the square next to the Spanish Steps, and had a spectacular terrace on which large trees seemed to grow, a building belonging to the Kaiser-Wilhelm Institute, where Herr Bruhns worked alongside other German art historians, on the façade of this building, too, there was the ugly black arrow pointing to the air-raid shelters,

and along the narrow, shadowy street, the bit of her journey that she liked the least, going into this gloomy street after the beauty of the Spanish Steps and the square with the obelisk in front of Trinità dei Monti,

the phrase *Enter ye in at the strait gate* came to mind, the maxim for January, and she could not help smiling at the fact that she thought of it here, after the bright, broad path she had trodden until this point, and that, too, was a miracle or a blessing, how the Bible always provided helpful and comforting words of encouragement for every circumstance in life, even for an afternoon stroll through Rome,

after every confinement there was space, after every darkness, light, after every emergency, help, but it was uncomfortable and exhausting and involved much sacrifice to obtain light and salvation, redemption and beatitude, that was more or less the meaning of this verse, everything was good, everything was in God's hands, and the more solid people were in this belief, the less they would be troubled by questions and anxieties, the more calmly they could wander down dark streets such as this,

the office where friendly Herr Bruhns worked must be behind one of these windows, there were so many friendly Germans here looking after her, because they had learnt of the tragic separation, as some said, of the young couple after only three days together, friends and acquaintances of her husband, who invited her for tea or spoke to her after church or passed by the deaconesses' mission and cheered her up by kind-heartedly enquiring as to how she was,

she liked listening to them talk about this city, they all knew each other and knew each other very well and, as they were not allowed to speak openly about the war or the situation in Germany, they discussed the inexhaustible subject of Rome and all there was to complain and admire about it,

obviously everybody had their own fixed opinion, their image of Rome, one would be interested almost exclusively in churches, the secretive Vatican and the silent Pope, the other would focus on antiquity and the Forum, the triumphal arches and the many emperors, some people admired the ornate architecture of the Baroque, others the new, sober, straight-line Mussolini buildings, some saw elegance and lightness everywhere, others laziness, sluggishness and ugliness, and only a few of them seemed to like or love this contradictory, impenetrable city of Rome in its entirety,

and neither had she ever met anyone who liked and esteemed the Romans, the Italians, except perhaps for Ilse, who preferred to chat with the washerwomen and ironers in the basement than hear reports of conversations with the wives of diplomats, envoys or attachés,

in general they looked down on the inhabitants of Rome, not openly and without contempt, but with the same matter-of-factness that they, in spite of all Christian love for one's neighbour, placed staff, servants, helpers and caretakers on a level below themselves,

as a silent observer in many conversations her impression was that even Italian professors, politicians or other people in positions of respect were more ridiculed than equivalent Germans, hence they sometimes smiled or made a little joke about the Duce, but never, ever about the Führer,

even she had been forced to admit that she found the Italians foreign, almost uncanny, the people she bumped into on the overly narrow pavements of Via Sistina, whether they were younger or older, women or men, most of them stepped aside for the pregnant woman, but did not appear

as if they wanted to further the understanding between the peoples of the two Axis powers, they did not behave as happily and high-spiritedly as one might expect of Italians, but rather indifferently or like disappointed conquerors whose national pride had taken a tumble, and if their faces, their eyes betrayed anything at all, it was the silent question: how much longer,

most were in a hurry or looked as if they were in a hurry, with their shopping bags or briefcases, nowhere in this lively city did you see two people standing together, chatting, as if this in itself was suspicious, inside a hardware shop two elderly gentlemen waited side by side at the door for customers, as stand-offish as guards, as if they were forbidden from letting anybody in,

since the ugly episode on the bus she had sought to create even more distance between herself and the Italians, and only ever got on a tram or bus if it was raining heavily, and although people would immediately offer her a seat when they saw her rounded belly, she preferred to walk, since that assault she had also lost the desire to write down Italian words in her vocabulary book, and at least to try to learn, and yet she felt happy walking down Via Sistina, free in the thought

that she did not have to join in the conversations with all the nice Germans who knew
so much about Rome, who knew each other and
gave each other recommendations about the few
preferred restaurants that received supplies, or
about the purchase of the few Italian specialities
that were still available, who seemed to have their
fixed opinions on Rome, the Romans, Italy and the
Italians, and who all behaved as if they had found
the key and solved the puzzle of Rome,

while she still found everything as puzzling
as the scene on the obelisk above the Spanish Steps,
the man, if it was a man, kneeling before the bird,
hieroglyphs or not, such images stuck, inexplicable,
heathen, images that could not be interpreted even
with verses from the Bible,

deep down she was relieved that she did
not have to join in this competition of Rome experts,
it did not bother her at all that she understood
Rome as little as she did that tiny picture on the
obelisk, she had no wish to be avidly cultured or
to have to appear avidly cultured, she did not wish
to be diverted from the two tasks she had, bringing
her child into the world, if that should be God's
will, and to be as close as possible to her husband
and to take him into her arms again as soon as
possible, if that should be God's will,

and she saw herself, *he who leaves all
power to God*, at the entrance to a pharmacy,

where a long mirror extended down to hip height, much larger than the mirror in the bathroom at the deaconesses' mission, she glanced at herself in her hat, and thought she looked almost too jaunty, too cheeky, too conspicuous, *will be wonderfully sustained by Him*,

but Gert liked it when she looked smart, as he said, *always dress well and behave, in all modesty, like a lady, so that they have respect for you*, and at that moment, as she saw herself with Gert's eyes, she in fact had respect for herself,

looked proudly at her belly and the narrow, fine, to her mind always too childish face, *like a Madonna painted by Perugino*, Gert had once said and shown her a postcard with an altarpiece by this painter and spoken of an uncanny similarity, vain thoughts, put them aside,

Via Sistina led straight ahead, first downwards, crossing the square with the human fish fountain, and then up into Via delle Quattro Fontane to the Wehrmacht headquarters, where she collected the letters from Africa, envelopes full of promise, without stamps but simple postmarks, signs of life carrying the field post number 48870 and

opened them, if not in a quiet corner, then on the street, and scanned the lines on the square paper before she read everything three or four times in peace at home and, if Ilse was not in the room, read the letter softly to her child, and it was her greatest and most secret pleasure when she felt the stirrings of a wordless answer inside her,

kept busy by strenuous work from six in the morning to midnight, Gert could usually only write short letters, or at night, when there was no more light, put down a few sentences by candlelight, and after reading these, she would commit at least one phrase to her memory until the next letter, so that some of his words stayed with her, went around with her, shone inside her day and night and in her dreams and in the morning,

as on this Saturday she carried round with her the words that were nine days old, nine days fresh from the letter she had received yesterday of 7th January, *Absorb all the beautiful things Rome has to offer, allow them right inside you, then the child will benefit too*,

and turned at the corner into Via Crispi, which rose steeply, right in front of her a knife-grinder jacked up his bicycle, set the grindstone going with his pedals, and began to sharpen a medium-sized kitchen knife, this old man looked almost identical to the knife-grinder who came every few weeks to Bismarckstrasse in Bad Doberan, everybody called him Fritz, Sharp Fritz, and she was on the verge of addressing his Roman counterpart in Low German dialect, into Via Crispi, where jewellers, tie shops and underwear shops displayed their sparse offerings in the windows, wedding rings of pale brass, as if they had been made from bullet casings, three dark ties beside a strange cap and the uniform of the Italian Hitler Youth, which obviously had a different name, but she did not know it, some vests and three discreetly folded pairs of knickers,

these shops with their almost empty shelves looked abandoned, people did not buy jewellery in wartime, and who still buys ties when starvation sits at one's table, at a pinch black ties for funerals, and perhaps there was still some business to be done selling warm underwear, given that most apartments were not heated,

perhaps thermal underwear was another thing only available on the black market, for everything that kept you warm, wool and cotton, was allocated to the soldiers in ice-cold Russia under the slogan *Wool for the Fatherland*, and private ownership of woollens was practically an act of treachery against the brave fighting troops of the Axis,

the street rose very steeply, and after a few strenuous strides the young woman turned right into Via degli Artisti, a narrower side street which also led uphill, and she tried to free her mind of these difficult, unpleasant thoughts, not exactly *all the beautiful things Rome has to offer*, by thinking of her beloved husband, who recently, in view of the difficult situation on the Russian front, had written to her quite openly, *how kindly God was to lead me, so that I ended up here and not there*, and who a year and a half ago had had the fortune to be wounded in the leg after only a few weeks of the Russian campaign, and was sent to military hospital, an unpleasant, prolonged affair of a wound that kept on reopening,

and which first of all saved him, as an infantry driver, from being sent back to the snow and the ice of the Russian front, where so many men had already fallen, and now entire companies were surrounded, and which allowed him, being lightly wounded, to perform some clerical work at headquarters in Rome, and to return finally to his calling and fulfil his duty in the pulpit, at the altar and at the baptismal font in Via Sicilia, which is what he should have been doing this winter too, with her to keep him company,

if yet another great battle had not been lost at El Alamein, with the result that, *for military reasons*, the army now also needed the reservists, those in reserved occupations, the lightly wounded, at least for the orderly rooms in Africa where his leg continued to afflict him and where he repeatedly consulted with doctors and staff surgeons over the correct therapy, and between the lines written on square paper expressed the hope that he might soon be sent back to Rome for better treatment for his leg,

where she, with healthy legs, only puffing a little and with a child flailing in her belly, climbed as if she were walking for Gert as well, who was not allowed to do much walking, past an open shop that repaired bicycles, and a white-haired carpenter who was just unlocking the door to his workshop, and who gave her a lengthy, surprisingly friendly look,

she needed her husband beside her and put all her hope in the injured leg, both of them wished, without being able to express this openly, for the wound to be bad enough for it to have to be treated in Rome, or in a military hospital in Italy, and yet not so serious that it could become really dangerous,

an inflammation of the cell tissue, the doctors said without knowing of a remedy, the glands swollen, but he could cope with the wound if there was no pain, as long as he was able to sit in the orderly room, it did not get worse, neither did it get any better, he just had to change the dressing and apply ointment every day, was not allowed to move much and could not visit the fabulous Roman ruins at Tunis along with his comrades,

just recently, more than a year since his deployment in Russia, he had been awarded the lowest of all honours, the Eastern Medal, for his injured leg, an honour so insignificant that it was to be handed out sometime after the war as the metal was required elsewhere, for now the award just consisted of a form letter and the ribbon,

in truth the wounded leg with its infection ought to be healing in a good military hospital, but so long as he was able to sit and type and telephone in Tunis, his superiors would not let him go, and could one be so selfish on account of a leg on which he could still walk and stand to some extent, betray one's comrades in Russia and in Africa, withdraw yet another man from the Wehrmacht and thus, she felt the overwhelming menace of such unwanted thoughts, perhaps imperil victory, the victory of the Axis Powers,

on the other hand, if his leg were to heal at some point, would he not be sent straight back to Russia, or to another bad front, it might mean the end of the fairly safe position in the orderly room in a villa on the outskirts of Tunis, where bombs fell only occasionally, but *the enemy is not so stupid as to drop his bombs on districts where there are lots of villas*,

who could tell, perhaps it would actually be better for him to stay on the African coast for the time being, *in relative safety*, where he had been summoned and ordered and still enjoyed the luxury of cooking himself a tinned sausage once a week in a real kitchen with a gas stove, who had the right to make that decision, you ought not to wish too much for yourself, ought not to expect too much, *everything is in God's hands, we will be patient and entrust everything to Him,*

she told herself whenever she became wrapped up in her own thoughts, and repeated these words again now, to calm herself, to resolve the complicated questions of the advantages and disadvantages of the leg issue, at least for the moment,

it would be a few minutes before she reached Via Sicilia, she looked along the street which led off to the right and to the human fish fountain, from up here the marble human fish, which she had often gazed upon out of helpless curiosity, could be seen from the side, the water rose out of the mussel shell he held and flowed down, *the stream rises and falls to fill,* this was not the right fountain either, which *Roman fountain* had the poet been thinking of,

why, in the capital of Christendom, were there these strange heathen figures everywhere, such as this human fish, the bird person, the fork gods, why was SPQR on every lamppost and every manhole cover, sometimes with full stops between the letters, sometimes without,

something Latin, Gert had explained to her, she had forgotten that too, and she did not dare to ask Frau Bruhns something so banal, who in Germany would believe her, Latin on the cast-iron manhole covers she walked over hundreds of times every day, over the sturdy iron with the capital letters S,P,Q,R, strange paths leading back two thousand years,

she sensed something within her rebelling against the constant obligation to stifle the feeling of longing with her reason and faith, because feelings were forbidden in wartime, you were not allowed to rejoice with happiness, you had to swallow your sadness, and like a soldier you were forced to conceal the language of the heart,

and the longing for the one who could answer such questions, who could allow her to develop a greater understanding and the appropriate sensitivity for the thousands of details of this attractive and repellent city in the shining splendour of its changing, surprising colours, she knew only too well,

who could reconstruct for her the ruins of the forums, complete the palaces and temples, translate the language of the stones, who could revive the vast number of fragments of the past, explain the pictures and sculptures of the fork gods and human fish, make the church ornaments radiate their brilliance, reconcile the contradictions between the heathen and the pious with delicate phrases, even in nondescript corners such as here, where your eyes could choose between looking right, down to Via Veneto with the fountain, or left towards a tranquil fenced garden with palms in front of a church for Irish monks,

she should not allow herself to feel this longing, it was not appropriate for a German soldier's wife, who ought to be waiting patiently at home, first for the final victory and then for her husband,

but she was not at home, she was in a foreign place, and carrying a child, she had thrown herself into an adventure, left her home and parents and followed her husband, without realizing that God had another plan for her, and nobody could expect her to stroll through this foreign place with a happy heart,

but in your distress and fear you can always take refuge in God's heart, you can have a good cry too, and beg Him repeatedly to give you a strong heart, beg that everything that comes from Him, even the most difficult trials, should be for the best,

she did not complain, she had not the slightest intention of complaining, she was *extremely fortunate*, all she was trying to do was to heed his advice, which he had given in his angular, not particularly legible handwriting, *absorb all the beautiful things Rome has to offer*, behind her secret tears she noticed time and again that it was much more difficult than he said, because out of sheer love he overestimated her and did not want to accept how helpless she felt in this labyrinth of the past, there were too many pasts at once,

and so, like a blossom that opens prematurely, this feeling of longing burst forth inside her again and again, more powerful than reason and military orders, and not everything that her throbbing heart whispered to her could immediately, that same moment, be held off and silenced by her faith in *Him, who brings order and rectitude to everything*,

on the pavement a man in a black shirt was blocking her path, he had turned his bicycle upside down and was trying to fit the chain back onto the sprockets, he did not seem to be having much success, he looked at his fingers blackened with oil and cursed, then he looked at her as if caught in the act and cursed again, she walked around him,

what comforted her was nature, the greenery in January, palms, cypresses, pines and agaves on a high garden terrace behind a four- or five-metre-high wall, she walked in the street beneath the laden boughs of these powerful trees, the wall must be a metre thick to bear and support all this,

she crossed to the right-hand side of the street, not because she was worried about an unstable wall, but to gain a better view of the green splendour around the multi-storey villa set on a hill, delighted by the yellow of the mimosas,

until at the next corner she came to a house whose ochre-brown façade was decorated with four stone putti, four chubby, winged boys hung on the corner wall, two supported and framed a coat of arms bearing the year 1889, below this a ribbon from which another boy hung, his head pointing downwards, holding onto a garland of fruits twice the size of himself, she could make out grapes, oranges, lemons and apples in the stone from which the fourth boy dangled,

the relief ran from the fourth down to the second storey of the house as far as the top of the balcony railings, which gave the impression of being a net for these daring artists, a cheerful scene, four gyrating, dancing putti, there was also something irritating about them with their candidly displayed, pointed genitals,

in about four weeks' time, she could not suppress this thought, you will see the sex of your child, she did not want to think about this so explicitly, and dampen the gratitude for the miracle growing and thriving inside her with obstinate, superfluous desires, whether it were a son or a daughter, that was God's will too, every child a gift, and they were as little agreed on girls' names as boys' names, and left up the street along the front of the steeply towering, chocolate-box villa, busy with hemispheres, columns, mouldings, recesses and statues, whose roof with its broad balustrades and vase finials contrasted with the soft, late-afternoon, winter blue of the sky, on most windows the matt-green shutters were down, perhaps the *palazzo* was no longer inhabited or difficult to heat, many rich Romans, people said, had moved to their country houses because of the air-raid warnings and poor food supplies,

the putti house was from 1889, almost the same year as the birth of her father, who would consider the stone-sculpted naked boys indecent, and find it hard to tolerate an encounter with a uniformed Fascist party member, cursing loudly over his bicycle, as well as the sight of this luxury villa and of Via Ludovisi, into which she now turned,

she had sometimes tried to imagine her father in Rome, a man who had had to live and grow up in such poverty, with such disciplined, God-inspired happiness, and such unassailable modesty to bring up six children and educate them as good Christians, but a former lieutenant commander and highly devout missionary like him was even less suited to this Catholic, wantonly beautiful excess,

particularly not in this area around Via Veneto with its gigantic, unaffordable hotels, restaurants and cafés, not even in his naval officer's uniform, which he had been wearing again since September 1939 to inspect the newly built or repaired warships in Kiel, before they were sent out into the battlefields of the oceans, although he would hardly stand out in this area of the city, in the hotels and the restaurants, because some German authorities had their headquarters here and German officers could occasionally be seen,

a man in a grey coat stood outside a shoe shop, cleaning his spectacles, but he appeared to be paying more attention to the reflecting pane of glass than to the shoes or his spectacles, a spy perhaps, she thought, *the Enemy is listening*, but what do spies look like, an Englishman perhaps, or an American, and what do Englishmen and Americans look like, she should move on quickly,

and just like her father she was not able to pass the luxurious buildings, resplendent with solemn colonnaded steps, magnificent balconies and elaborately decorated windows with opulent sills, without wondering who could afford, or still afford to live, dine or drink the ridiculously expensive coffee here, which was not to be found anywhere else,

but she had to admit that this was only an assumption, a prejudice, perhaps behind these windows adorned with flowers or beneath the domed tower of the Hotel Excelsior, which she was now approaching, they only drank tea or orange juice or wine, or the commonplace substitute coffee in precious gilt-edged cups,

every time she walked to church she grappled with the mystery of who might be filling these many hotels in the fourth year of the war, and for whom these uniformed porters, always ready for service and proud of their colours and braids, were opening doors and whistling for taxicabs, there were no foreign tourists, the rich were living in the countryside, what remained were businessmen, the military and party bigwigs from Germany, Italy and Japan, and perhaps spies after all,

as she crossed Via Veneto a brief glance to the right, where the street wound its way down in elegant curves to the human fish fountain and to the fountain of the bees, and a good, long look to the left, to the far end of the avenue, at the gates of the ancient Roman city wall, there was a distant radiance of venerability in the reddish brown of the ancient tiles,

a wall that had once been built, as Gert explained to her, to protect the Romans from us, the barbarians, roughly in those centuries in which Feliz Dahn's *A Struggle for Rome* was set, which she had read, on Gert's recommendation, in preparation for her visit, walls were no longer needed these days, today Romans and Germans stood together as close allies in an axis against the rest of the hostile world,

and on the way up Via Veneto, past Hotel Excelsior, she encountered elegant ladies and gentlemen and made-up young women, and in such proximity to the riddles of that wealth hidden behind hotel walls, almost in contact with them, she felt the joy of a deep gratitude that this was not her world, and that she had a man at her side who was unimpressed by all of this, and a father who had taught her humility,

because he had always had it tough himself, raised as the third son on a Mecklenburg farm until his own father fell from a horse that had taken fright in a storm and could no longer work, paralyzed in a wheelchair, and so had to sell the farm which owed debts in any case, and soon died, while his mother, depressed by the misery of this ill luck, was sent to an institution for the mentally disturbed and locked up for life and

from the age of ten he and his two brothers were drilled, one after the other, at cadet school until he, the youngest, because he was perceptibly small, wanted to show himself to be the bravest of all and signed up for the dreaded, notoriously severe navy, and in his marine-blue uniform

rose to the rank of submarine captain when the Great War broke out, sunk ships for his beloved Kaiser and, with a terribly bad conscience, watched the seamen from the sinking enemy cruisers and frigates plummet into the sea, while many of his closest comrades drowned, one of his brothers crashed as a pilot and the other fell in the trenches in France, and in the end he stood there not only without family and without Kaiser, without whom his life had become meaningless, but also without an occupation,

married, one child, soon two, and failed just as badly as an assistant gardener as he did as an apprentice at the Mecklenburg hailstorm and fire insurance company, and became seriously ill with unaccountable paralysis until God saved him and appointed him to be a travelling preacher who sought to lead people along the path to faith with the power of his captain's voice in lectures such as 'What Does Love Mean?' or 'The Deepest Human Value' or 'How Do We Cope with Life?'

and who would have seen nothing but sin here, in the splendour of Via Veneto, amongst perfumeries, jewellers and first-rate gentlemen's tailors, and perhaps the only thing in the whole of Rome he would have warmed to would have been the painting depicting the conversion of Paul in the Lutheran church in Piazza del Popolo, because conversion and calling, Job and Paul were the central themes of his life, and because he would have been able to equate Paul's fall from his horse

with his father's fall, the Bible with life, and would
have drawn his lessons from this, and

she, too, the second-born daughter, sometimes felt too Evangelical or too North German or
too young in the city they called Eternal, as if being
here were contrary to her actual nature, and then
she got the feeling that it was not right to wander
around as a German amongst the Romans in the
middle of the war, just because she was waiting
for her husband, to step over the manholes with
the letters SPQR and GAS and the black basalt
paving slabs,

and that perhaps it was not right to enter
any part of this beautiful, foreign country, or to
measure it with military steps or to transform it
into a mere parade ground as the German officers
had done with such a casualness that it was
almost provocative, those officers who posed for
photographs in front of the Colosseum or the ruins
of the Forum, or sat here at the corner in Café
Doney, as if they intended to stay for ever, and who
appeared to feel at ease with their glass of wine
or beer in the late afternoon, as if they were the
masters here and not the guests,

well-to-do Italians, so far as she in passing
could identify them by their clothes, gestures and
poise, also sat at some of the tables, never more
than four people, as was the case everywhere else,
to begin with this had amazed her, because the

Italians had always been portrayed as a sociable people who sat at long tables, took great pleasure in eating and drinking to the accompaniment of mandolin-playing street singers,

until Ilse told her that Mussolini had issued a directive stipulating that no more than four people were allowed to sit together at a restaurant or café table, because the authorities evidently feared that larger groups might give rise to conspiratorial thoughts,

so many directives demanding things of you in wartime, and which were no doubt necessary as far as maintaining general discipline and order were concerned, idlers were undesirable, and yet here you saw people who looked like idlers, make-up was frowned upon, and yet in this area you came across made-up women,

perhaps there were just too many laws and regulations, the number of people allowed to sit at a table, the way you had to greet each other and dress and behave, who had to be hated and who you had to put your hope in, what you had to eat and read and listen to and know,

at the same time the Italians had been loyal to their Duce, and had rejoiced as they followed him with banners, deployments and conquests in the first missions of the war, it was similar to the enthusiasm of the Germans for their Führer, but for about twice as long as the Germans, for more than twenty years now they had shared in their country's elevation to an empire and the pride this had generated, and they had extolled the uniformed benediction of Fascism from the construction of housing to the punctuality of the trains and the peace and order on the streets empty of beggars and invalids, even in the Via Veneto of the wealthy,

but the war, Frau Bruhns had said recently, *the war is going on too long for them, people only like war if it is young, and for the Italians the war is feminine,* la guerra, *whereas for us Germans it is masculine, people only idolize young women, do you understand what I'm saying,*

then Frau Bruhns had stopped talking, and the idea of the war, which was supposed to be feminine, had remained hanging in the air, beneath the pines of Ostia Antica, of course she had not said anything either, she did not say much at the best of times, particularly not in the company of such educated people, she would not have known how to add to this observation or what to ask whether war was feminine or masculine,

she turned into Via Sicilia, the thought that the war pleased nobody any longer made her feel uneasy, unfortunately it had not yet been won, and luckily not yet lost, but in all probability people were tired of the many deaths, fresh defeats, separations and directives, orders, sirens, threats, pains, sleeplessness, rationing and the supplies that dwindled each month,

but one must not harbour those thoughts, and she, in particular, must not harbour those thoughts, as a German and the wife of a soldier fighting in Africa, in any case she must not think so much, she had to carry, protect and nourish the child, that was her task, the most wonderful task a woman could have,

almost there, just two more turnings before she reached the church she was walking to, as she did every Sunday, the island of salvation in the Roman ocean, where she was safe from all temptations, including such rebellious thoughts about the war,

which she must shake off as quickly as possible, they had probably only occurred to her because, apart from the sisters of the deaconesses' mission and four or five women from the German colony and community, she only had Ilse to talk to, who, with her stories from the kitchen and laundry,

professed to understand the modern Romans and preferred to talk about the comet that could be seen this year in the constellation of the Great Bear and was supposed to signify some future event, rather than abide, with Christian humility and faith in the Lord, by the maxim for January, *Enter ye in at the strait gate*, this was a clearer message than that of the stars and comets, at the start of Via Sicilia, two houses behind Via Veneto, a poster in black capital letters, faded by the sun and rain to grey, pasted to a forgotten billboard, advertising a performance in March 1941 of Christoph Willibald Gluck's *Orfeo ed Euridice* by the Berlin Staatsoper at Rome's Teatro Reale,

every time she went to church this old poster reminded her of the days shortly before her engagement in October '40, when Gert and she had heard *Orpheus und Eurydike* in Kassel Opera House and had been so enraptured by the blissful music that afterwards they hummed the tune *She is gone, and gone for ever*, at the time when they had just found each other, could regard everything as a game, and were still able to joke about separation,

March '41, barely two years ago, four months before the wedding, before the Russian war, before the war in Africa, all that seemed in the distant past, almost as peacetime did, and for this reason she was always pleased that the poster was still on display there, and had not been pasted over or ripped down, and that it evoked her happiness, the beginning of her still ongoing happiness, and

she approached the church with joyful steps, no longer paying attention to the shop windows, the empty restaurants and the people coming towards her, she went up to the church, whose bright frontage, which became more clearly visible from the side with every step, stood out against the profiles of the neighbouring houses along the length of the street, all that was missing was the ringing of the bells, why should they not ring for a church concert too,

with joyful steps, the way she had always gone to Bible study and services, apart from between the ages of thirteen and fifteen, when she was completely taken by the League of German Girls, and the handbook *Girls on Duty* had pushed the hymn book and the Christian scriptures into the background but, nevertheless, she

obeyed the summons of her father and of the bells as a confirmand in Doberan, as a young girl at the housewifery school in Kassel, and at the kindergarten teacher-training college in Eisenach, sometimes uneasy, sometimes dissatisfied with herself, as when she was a kitchen assistant at the Lazarus hospital in Berlin, and yet church doors had only rarely felt too narrow or pews too hard, and she had always found something uplifting in the songs, liturgies and sermons, a comforting adage or verse and a firmer heart,

and a vital balance to the hostility of the League of German Girls' leaders towards Christianity, and that of the Führer himself who, as her father and Gert sometimes cautiously hinted, made the mistake of placing himself above God, or practically allowing himself to be venerated as a god, and so exaggerated the belief in race and the superiority of the German national community,

You are nothing, your people is every-thing!, that the racial theories contradicted ever more sharply the obligations of humility and brotherly love, and repeatedly gave rise to fresh inner conflicts in young people like her,

without the Church and her devout parents and several courageous preachers she would not have been able to cope with the daily conflict between the cross of the Church and the crooked cross of the swastika, between the *selfless community* of the League of German Girls and the *selfless community* of the Christians and

would not have been able to achieve the difficult balance between the wonderful times around the camp fire with competent, uniformed girls, the fun games and social evenings, the singing and physical exercises, the instruction in racial theory, national customs, first aid, nature, and the zeal for *serving the people and fatherland*, on the one hand,

and on the other, the Bible study which her mother gave at home to a dozen girls from her class and that of her sister, Christian teaching, and the unwavering captain's voice of her father,

with which he would strike up, in the face of the dangers, temptations and adversities of the world, his *Praise to the Lord, the Almighty, the King of creation* or *A mighty fortress is our God*, early in the morning if possible, her father who knew how to defend himself at every turn with hymns, and who, it seemed, *Even if the earth were full of devils*, nothing could alarm any more,

since he, in despair at the collapse of the empire and the Bolshevik workers' uprisings after the war, or due to a malicious virus, first developed problems walking and then his legs and voice became paralyzed, an illness with a high fever lasting for days, so baffling that the doctors had given up on him,

until very gradually the paralysis abated, disappearing completely after about six months, during which time the two of them, her mother and her father, recognized that their Christianity had only been a formality and not a real commitment, so from that point on together they prayed, sang and praised God with loud voice, who had saved the father so miraculously at the time of his greatest need, as He had once saved Job,

so after all these trials the life of her father had become one long service, and he himself a preacher who went to meetings of workers, communists and Nazis, in order to lead them away from political ideas and win them for heavenly salvation, and he proselytized to the people in pubs, tents and churches, attempting to guide them onto the one right path, consultations in the morning, Bible study in the afternoon, lectures in the evening, until the new powers banned this work soon after the Olympics,

with joyful steps approached the church that meant far more to her than the other places of worship she had been to in the past, because this was the only place in Rome, besides the deaconesses' mission in Via Alessandro Farnese, where she not only understood every word, but longed for them and welcomed them, where she was addressed in the language familiar to her, in a well-phrased German which warmed her heart and soul, and where hymns, prayers and blessings provided strength for everyday life and

strength to endure the separation from her husband, who really should have been performing his duty here, speaking from the pulpit in his voice, if there were no war, or at least only a minor war, in which there was no need for theologians with wounded legs in orderly rooms in Africa,

for this reason the comfort she received here was doubled, trebled, without the Lutheran Gospel she would not have been able to cope with Rome and would hardly have been able to leave the house, in spite of Dr Roberto's encouragement, *Walk, young lady, walk*, almost as paralyzed as her father had once been, she felt this very plainly, and without the energy she regained here each week she would not have been able to carry the entire

Wartburg in her head through the streets of Rome

or the familiar Doberan Minster, whose outline appeared to her now, during these last few metres, the warm tone of bright-red brick, the music of majestically tall windows, the row of steep arches in the most slimline Cistercian Gothic, the slate roof with its pencil-tip tower, in the middle of the green countryside, amongst meadows and trees and near-derelict monastery walls, the Minster stood in the limpid Baltic air,

to which she had walked in a wide arc, arm in arm with her beloved husband, she in a bridal dress, he in a borrowed dinner suit, and the entire large family behind them, here on Via Sicilia by the Lutheran church she wished she could feel the pressure and the warmth of his right arm, as she had felt it back then during their wedding procession towards the south portal,

when everything was good, and God's will was her will, to follow this man wherever he went, first of all into this centuries-old, astonishingly beautiful church, familiar to her since childhood with its woodcut, strangely vivid and radical Bible figures at the main altar, the lions on the pew ends and the naked figures of Adam and Eve with the crowned serpent, and, beneath the richly decorated vaults, near the portraits of the rulers of Mecklenburg, pillars with bright ornaments and the huge monumental crucifix, to say to him, I will, since then she sometimes felt that with each church visit, whether it be in Doberan or Rome, she was also confirming the *I will* she had uttered to him a year and a half earlier, when the order to *prepare for deployment* had already been given, and all the guests knew

that soon after the wedding night he would have to leave to conquer Russia, Moscow, and half of the family shared the silent fear that they would soon see the bride a widow at nineteen or, if fate were to be more merciful, pitched at twenty from white into black like so many,

now she had followed him to the friendly foreign land, at the junction with Via Toscana by the church, concert-goers, individuals or in pairs, appeared, some nodded to her, others, such as Frau Fondi, Frau Heymann and Frau Toscano, who she knew better, offered their hand, but not Frau von Mackensen, the wife of the ambassador, who had just got out of a black Mercedes and had helped arrange her visa for Italy, Gert had said, and who she was always slightly afraid of, because the ambassador was such an important man,

most of them looked at her belly in acknowledgement and smiled at her, people knew her because people knew her husband here, they were pleased that a German woman would soon be giving birth to another German child in Via Alessandro Farnese, they were all nice to her, all of them in a peaceful mood beneath the figure of Christ which, flanked by Peter and Paul above the entrance, awaited visitors and seemed to say, *Come unto me, all ye that labour and are heavy laden*, while she looked around for Schwester Luise and Schwester Ruth, who were to accompany her on the journey home, and who she wished to sit next to, and suddenly,

as if she had heard a call from afar, looked back in the direction of Via Veneto at the evening sky above the street, the roof gardens and the reddish-gold glimmer on the clouds of the red western sky, it was the view towards the south, towards Africa, but she was sure that at this very moment Gert was also looking in the direction of the setting sun, thinking the same as her, only then did she

climb the steps, shake hands again in the narthex, and receive more good wishes from people, even those she only knew by sight, and she felt as if these people, by bidding the young pregnant woman welcome, were trying to give themselves some hope in these tough days of losses and defeats,

while two girls, probably confirmands, handed out the programmes for the concert which ought to have taken place on the 8th of November, but had to be postponed at the last minute because heavy bombing had meant that the oratory singer, Albrecht Werner from Stuttgart, had not been able to get to the railway at Innsbruck on time, and so the concert had been rearranged for this Saturday, with the old printed programmes from 8th November 1942,

and she entered the church and first looked for the white hoods of the deaconesses, the church was quite full, in the first row she recognized Frau von Bergen, the wife of the ambassador to the Vatican, to whom she had already paid her respects, everywhere people sought the proximity of friends and acquaintances, the shaking of hands and nodded greetings continued inside the church,

the two sisters, easy to recognize by their hoods, were already seated, they had kept a place for her in one of the middle rows, and finally, after almost an hour of leisurely walking, she was able to sit down, sit down carefully and shift the weight inside her body, she immediately felt such relief in her legs and feet, in her shoulders and in her over-burdened spine, that she let out a sigh, which caused Schwester Luise to give her a look of concern,

no, she told herself, unbuttoning her coat, it was not too much, *Walk, young lady, walk*, every step, she had enjoyed every single step, but a longer walk would have been too much, it was precisely the right distance, she did not feel exhausted, it was just the desire finally to sit down and breathe more easily, nothing more, everything was as it should be, everything was fine, she began to get excited about the organ, the choir, the singer and the string quartet,

as she looked straight ahead at the glinting mosaic tiles in the apse, where Jesus sat enthroned on a blue planet and a rainbow, his right hand raised in the greeting of benediction, in his left the script with the letters alpha and omega, clad in a gold-and-white cloth robe, folded many times over, this mighty figure before a background of sparkling golden mosaic tiles in an oval wreath of floral ornaments,

it was as if the saviour, with his eyes and gestures, was demanding silence from above, people had stopped whispering and murmuring, Pfarrer Dahlgrün stepped forward and greeted the audience, spoke of the vicissitudes of war and of the gratitude with which the community was finally receiving this concert today, he kept it short, avoided speaking as if it were a service, and did not recite the Lord's Prayer,

perhaps he did not want to annoy the Italian, the Catholic music lovers who, given the scarcity of opportunity, had come to listen once more to Bach or a Haydn string quartet, or simply to listen to nothing but music for an hour, German music, mainly Baroque music, both instrumental and choral, perhaps this time the pastor just wanted to allow the harmonies of the chorales and soloists and string players to convey the message, as there were hardly any concerts any more, not in the evenings due to the air-raid warnings, and in the afternoons people had other things to do, once in December she had been lucky enough to see *Der Rosenkavalier*, Frau Heyman had offered her a press ticket for the dress rehearsal, unfortunately she had understood nothing as it was sung in Italian, nonetheless she was grateful for a musical experience and the beautiful voices,

Schwester Luise had also said it was a miracle that this concert was taking place at all, who knows when we might have something like this again, a miracle that the railway line was not bombed this time, a miracle that string quartets and choirs could even still meet to practise, led by Frau Fürst, in charge of the community's music, who engaged them to appear at these concerts and who also played the organ,

and with full force, it was almost frightening, the organ started up with chords which first shot like thunderbolts into the soul and limbs, and then filled the room with a cheerful, ordered arrangement that dominated everything, and even woke the child in her belly, which wriggled as if wanting to join in, dance along or at least listen and feel with the rest of the audience,

she smiled and leant back in order to think of nothing except for the wriggling of her child and the joyously leaping piped notes of the prelude, leant back to relax and be carried along by the clear melodies and broken harmonies, and when these pleasures were over far too quickly, she attempted to retain in her ears for as long as possible the last chord that floated and faded in the room,

after a short break the organ started up again, complemented by the choir which stood in the gallery behind the audience, *I call to Thee, Lord Jesus Christ*, unlike many in the front rows she did not turn around, it was strange to be in a concert where the music reached your ears from behind, but that was no reason to gawp backwards and upwards,

she found it perfectly natural to join in quietly with the chorale, just to herself, without raising her voice, and sing along, calling out and asking for help, *Bestow me with grace at this time*, and, with each bar, the inner feeling of uncertainty or anxiety she sometimes had, her Roman anxiety, was lifted away layer by layer, *that I may no more be scorned*, like a soft, harmonious prayer, *give me hope as well*, while she

stared at the mosaic of the face of Jesus, not as delicately worked as the very early mosaic faces, such as those in Santa Prassede, which Gert had shown her, here everything was somewhat cruder and the splendour more laboured, she looked at the beard and the strikingly large hands and feet, without scars, and the arabesques of vine leaves and grapes on both sides branching out in all directions, and in which her floating, aimless thoughts and wishes became entangled, and to the right of that,

looked at the eagle lectern in the stone pulpit, embedded with reliefs of the prophets and apostles, and suddenly, or finally, she understood why in this city she kept noticing sculptures, ornaments and images of eagles and, with a feeling of relief, she allowed her gaze to rest on the elevated pulpit,

where her husband ought to be standing and from where she had yet to hear him preach, there the wings and head of a marble eagle supported a panel and an angled board made out of dark wood for Bibles, manuscripts, notes, only now did she remember that the eagle was the symbol of John the Evangelist, this eagle of John was more ancient and more important than all state or Borghese eagles, than the eagles with the swastika or

fasces, and more beautiful as well, with its bearing, helping, useful wings, not as domineering or burly or luxuriant as the other stone eagles,

although not for the first time she felt confused here by the quotation on the pulpit GOD'S WORD WITH US IN ETERNITY, which sounded almost the same as the words on the soldiers' buckles GOD WITH US, both were right and yet somehow did not go together, on the belt the eagle with the swastika, on the pulpit the eagle with vines, and she was unable to resolve her confusion in this matter,

until the soloist, Herr Werner who had travelled from Stuttgart, stood on the steps by the altar and, accompanied only by the cello, filled the tall room with his voice, with the aria 'You Have Fear in the World', met the sensibilities of the audience and at the same time was able to offer consolation with his warm, paternal bass tones,

a voice that she was happy to listen to and which, in spite of its powers of consolation, she found disquieting, arousing a longing for the male voice, the bass she missed, she must not complain, she must not yearn too deeply, *how much nicer it would be if we were not at war*, Gert had written in his New Year's letter, *but given that we are at war, we are very fortunate... to remain protected from all harm... so many lovely hours*,

yes, this was a lovely hour, she was *incredibly lucky*, she received her letters fairly regularly, she had his photograph, from morning till evening she felt his presence in her child and in all her thoughts and feelings, but his voice was missing, she became immediately aware of this, for nine weeks she had not heard his voice speak, whisper, sing, not a long time, compared with the experiences of other soldiers' wives or that of Ilse, but far too long nonetheless, and in spite of all her self-control tears started to flow, she resisted them in vain,

and still more tears when the bass sang the second Bach aria, 'Yea Though I Walk in Death's Dark Vale', the variation on Psalm 23, again with the cello that swept through the depths of the soul, the tears flowed, she reached for a handkerchief, wiped her cheeks and held back her sobs, so as not to disturb the singer, yet could not stop weeping, Schwester Luise took her arm, stroked her hand, and she felt ashamed, because her tears came so readily and simply refused to stop,

even as a child she had cried more than her five siblings, she had grown up with the saying, *built close to water*, even for a girl it was a stigma to burst into tears and howl on account of trivial things,

something not even her captain father with his continually repeated admonitions such as *Spare the tears, later on you will have more reason to cry*, was able to stop, especially not with jokes such as *Dearest Liese, weep you not, not every bullet hits the spot*, for how could the sobbing child know how many harmful bullets flew through life and which ones you had to watch out for,

the consolations of the *staff and rod*, which the bass sang emphatically, were of more help, as was the overwhelming final chorale of the

St Matthew Passion, where for once crying was not forbidden, but was part of the power of the sorrow, *We sit down and weep*, which is why once she had heard this section in Doberan Minster, she loved and treasured it like no other piece by Bach, and she would summon it whenever she was most ashamed of her tears in an attempt to mobilize all her powers of resistance,

not until the end of the aria with the meander through the comforting psalm, during the Haydn C major string quartet, played by four Italians, did the tears stop, she caught her breath, the *dark vale* had been traversed, she had regained her composure, and after the first, lively, cheerful movement,

she felt liberated and happy and, to focus her mind on something different, she read the names of the musicians from the programme, Corrado Archibugi, Gino Giometti, Clemente Pagliassotti, Marco Peyot, she was sure that she would mispronounce them all, but that did not bother her,

as now, while allowing her eyes to wander over the slabs of marble on the walls, over the grey, red, brown, black and white, and the different patterns of the most exquisite marble paid for by Kaiser Wilhelm, and while the strings created a detached mood with the second, slow movement, she tried to picture a future without war, without air-raid warnings, orders to keep one's chin up, without the scarcely comprehensible differences between *orders to muster*, *orders to detach* and *orders to march*, a future without Wehrmacht reports, without enemies and without quarrels, without the deaths that could no longer be tallied, and the daily death announcements *Fallen in action*, which were printed ever smaller,

without the young men far away in foreign lands, and the mothers and children in burning cities, without the overcrowded hospitals and field hospitals, without amputations, shots in the head, frostbite and leg ulcers, without rationing at starvation levels and shortages even in Rome, and without Ilse's depressing reports from the washerwomen and cooks and without the superstitions about comets,

tried to picture a May-green future far away, in the Reich, a friendly home with Gert, who as a war orphan had never had a real home, with the child, with four or six children, preferably in a village somewhere, maybe a timber-framed house with a garden in Hessen, where he came from, perhaps a thatched house in Mecklenburg with the sea air, it did not matter, just so long as it was not in the city,

most of all, peace and a life without trep-idation or worries in the tranquil rhythm of the church year with organs and bells and singing, as in Röhrda near Kassel, where Gert's brother was the pastor, and where they had spent a wonderful holiday the previous May,

and she tried to picture quiet evenings without the wailing of sirens, with swallows at sunset, a bench in front of the house where they could happily sit side by side, watching the children run around and play, and if they were really lucky, perhaps listen later to this very Haydn string quartet on the radio,

she found it difficult to imagine all this, even though the violins, the viola and the cello encouraged such thoughts with the truculent Haydn cadences, especially the allegretto movement, which in the church seemed almost cheeky, she found it difficult to remove herself from the God-given present with such immense, almost blasphemous leaps, it was hard enough to look back, for example to the date 8th November, the date printed on the programme,

she had not yet arrived in Rome, she had just obtained her visa and packed her cases by the Baltic, back then the situation was a little better on the fronts in Africa and in Russia, in Stalingrad, the name now on everybody's lips, and the German cities were less damaged then,

even this most recent past, the beginning of November, with all its hopes in the *Roman delights*, now seemed to her relatively peaceful, in retrospect each past appeared more peaceful than the present, for example the walk with Gert up to the Wartburg and their engagement in October 1940 seemed from today's perspective almost like peacetime, while their wedding summer of 1941 was much more peaceful than autumn 1942,

and perhaps in a year's time she would think back to this Saturday in January 1943 and reflect with envy how peaceful it was when, in good health and pregnant, she had walked through the winter warmth of Rome and listened to a concert while giving free rein to her fantasies for the future with a husband who was still alive,

no, she must not think too much about all of that, must not expect or wish for too much, the future was in the hands of the one pictured in the golden mosaic giving the blessing and pointing gently at the Bible, but sometimes she had to be allowed to dream of a life after the war, which her housewife instruction and the kindergarten teacher-training college had prepared her for, prepared as a mother and a wife at the side of the husband destined for her,

you also had to pray for a happy finale, which the strings seemed to promise most beautifully with their artistry, and for this you had to pass *through the strait gate*, even though this gate was not at all narrow, nor difficult, nor did you have to walk crouched, but, when the time came, upright and with your head raised humbly, to bring your own will into harmony with the will of God, and thereby find the greatest freedom in obedience,

applause, suddenly there was applause when the string quartet came to an end, there is no applause in church, not in the Evangelical Church, neither the organist, nor the choir, nor the solo singer had been applauded, it was more of a Roman Catholic tradition to clap in church, even at funerals, but here, following the chorales and arias, the applause sounded even more insubordinate than the worldly music that had strayed far beyond the usual practices of praising and thanking, and had triumphed over day-to-day worries,

the music which had evidently stirred or reinforced the longing for peace amongst other members of the audience too, perhaps people were showing their gratitude for the liberating impulse of their dearest and innermost fantasies, possibly provoked by the final chords of the Italian string players, full of joy for peace, and played with such great effect,

perhaps it was the Catholics or concert lovers who had burst into applause out of habit after the fourth movement, and then the others had joined in, even she had sheepishly put her hands together a few times before she realized what she was doing, and then it was all over, over much too quickly,

and in the two-minute break, while the string players left their seats, there was restlessness in the audience, occasional whispers could be heard, a moment of embarrassment, hopefully Frau Fürst, who had put the programme together and certainly not planned for this Haydn piece to have such a liberating effect on the audience, would not have any trouble from the *official people* who, either in uniform or civilian clothes, must be sitting everywhere, not just in the front rows,

especially Frau Fürst, who lived for music alone and who, with the words *open up your heart to music!*, never tired of inviting everybody she met to join the singing group, and encouraged their active participation in trying to unite musically with the Almighty,

a link the bass singer now sought to forge again with the solo part 'I Laid Me down and Slept, I Awaked' by Heinrich Schütz, he had a difficult task singing against the unsettling restlessness of the congregation inside the church, which surprised itself with its behaviour, moreover the piece of music he had to perform was more delicate, and the text more disturbing, *My God, thou hast smitten all mine enemies upon the cheek bone, thou hast broken the teeth of the ungodly,* it did not fit with Haydn's lovely harmonies, and neither did it relate to Germany's enemies, the British, Americans and French, who after all were Christians too, it could only mean the Bolsheviks, if it was appropriate to apply the biblical message to the present, the battles against the Russians were the hardest and most costly, and the outcome not yet decided, even though, from the very first, the Führer had fought and almost defeated communism, this religion of the ungodly,

perhaps the *official people* were now satisfied that the war morale had been weakened only momentarily in this concert and Heinrich Schütz had reinforced it again, whereas she, seated next to the sighing Schwester Luise, did not want to think about it, certainly not in the middle of a wonderful concert,

so instead she looked at the font where she and Gert hoped to have their child baptized in a few weeks' time, something she had difficulty imagining just then, instead she continued her daydream of an unknown future with her family living somewhere in the country,

when the war and the separation were over, she saw herself coming gladly to Rome again with Gert, to visit the deaconesses' mission, to enjoy those pleasures together that he had once rhapsodized about, the exceptional ice cream, the ridiculously cheap, juicy oranges, the fat cherries in May, the chocolate, the bitter coffee that could only be drunk with lots of sugar, and maybe even the elaborate, very long spaghetti with over-spicy sauces, and at last learn how to turn her fork properly while eating it,

wander hand in hand through the Forum and over the Palatine Hill and through the old streets, rest a while in the silent Pantheon and raise their faces in gratitude, warming themselves in the kind morning sun or the benevolent evening sun, or beneath parasols on terraces where officers were now sitting, and look and marvel,

Oh how fleeting, oh how slight, the choir began, accompanied powerfully by the organ, catch up on everything, the museums, starting with the gallery in the Borghese park, and let Gert show her everything again in peace, the fork gods and Caesar and Augustus and Michelangelo, and

descend into the catacombs, where the first Christians survived centuries of persecution and where she did not dare venture on her own, or where it was too risky for a woman in her eighth month of pregnancy, steep, slippery steps, she had heard, and arduous bus journeys along the potholed roads of the outer suburbs,

she would rather save these adventures for a better time with Gert, *Oh how fleeting, oh how slight*, again the organ seemed to induce the child to kick out, and go on the trips that other people had gushed to her about, to the gardens in Tivoli, to the vineyards of Frascati, *are the days of human life*, to the sea at Ostia, or by tram up to Monte Cavo, *as a stream begins to flow*,

destinations which to her, richly endowed with the sights of Rome, seemed like a double, even triple luxury, as if the bottomless wealth of the city were not enough, as if you always had to surpass beauty with new beautiful things, as if you could not be content with what you had, *and pauses not as it runs on*, difficult thoughts which, if her much longed-for husband were here, she might be able to discuss, or perhaps they would all of a sudden become irrelevant,

if now, because of his injured leg, he were simply to fly back across the sea to Naples, and then take the train, *and pauses not as it runs on*, she would not have to wait for some distant peacetime to go with him to Monte Cavo or Tivoli, perhaps in spring already, after the birth, she might be able to go with him and the child to the beach at Ostia, in the sand and sun, *so our time drifts away*, family outings such as those she used to make to Heiligendamm,

from the eyes of the Christ figure en-throned in the golden mosaic heaven, from the bearded face beneath the halo she read this gentle exhortation not to wish for too much nor indulge in idle fantasies, she concentrated, the climax of the afternoon was imminent, the cantata 'I Will Gladly Bear the Cross', now the soloist stood up again, the string players, standing in for the orchestra, tuned their instruments, the organ gave the concert pitch, the choir hummed,

and then the singer, accompanied by the strings, let his bass stream forth, firmly, confidently, every word intoned with integrity and joy, and the most beautiful thing was how he could sustain, raise, lower and smooth the pitch on the word *bear* for so long, without a breath, or with only a scarcely audible one, that *bear* seemed to be a musical depiction of the long and patient act of bearing, a piece of virtuosity the singer repeated with the same sequence of notes for the word *care*,

she could almost sing along silently to the slow aria, and just as she took every word from the Bible as assistance and encouragement, this too went straight to her soul, the music of Bach penetrated to the very depths of her soul, inspired by biblical and other powerful phrases and by the clear sight of a beseeching and thanking I,

which was also her I, which found its own thoughts expressed in every sung syllable, *my Redeemer wipes my tears away*, that is exactly how it had just been, but she could never have put it so beautifully, perhaps she might not have been able even to think it, astonished at the miracle that, with a single cantata, this Johann Sebastian Bach, two hundred years after his time, could understand and express the feelings of a twenty-one-year-old woman, highly pregnant and alone, cast away from the Baltic to the Mediterranean, in limbo in the middle of a terrible war, and could soothe her, but not just her,

no doubt everybody here could relate what they were hearing to their own lives, to the war and hardship, and to the everyday reality of death, no doubt Frau Fürst had chosen cantata number 56 for this very reason, for an audience in which everyone had already lost close relatives and friends and was adjusted to death,

she could be grateful that everybody in her immediate family was still alive, her parents, her five siblings, and Gert's only brother, and she prayed that it may stay like this, it had been much worse in the last war, then two of her father's brothers and one of her mother's had not returned, as well as dozens of cousins and uncles and friends of her parents, Gert's father had died prematurely, and soon after the war his mother had died too, and many more from that family had died far too young,

but precisely because they were all still alive, the probability that one would fall victim grew with every day, it might be her siblings and parents, it might happen to all of them today, perhaps not in peaceful Rome, who could tell, not in Rome yet,

how long would she be able to stay, if the fronts started to move and the Americans and British got closer in North Africa, the sea to Sicily is not that wide, and they will not spare the Eternal City from bombs for all eternity, and what will happen to Mussolini, if some of Ilse's fears or secret hopes were true, and yet,

she did not want to worry, and so she abandoned herself again to the bass voice and the cello, *in the Lord shall I find strength*, and it seemed to her as if the power of this music delivered itself to her, as if the melodies were building a protective wall,

higher and more magnificent, as if they were rising and forming an architectural structure with high vaults, *and with the wings of the eagle*, and she felt secure in this music as if she were in a pantheon of notes, *shall I fly away from this earth*, beneath a heavenly ladder made of pure heavenly scales, and beneath a dome of harmonies,

beneath which her life fitted and both their lives and that of the child, and beneath which, brightly elevated by recitative and arioso, the Wartburg and Doberan Minster slotted into place, the Pincio and the Jacob's ladder at the Spanish Steps, and mighty Rome in her entirety, which she no longer feared, and beneath which even the war seemed to shrink,

beneath a dome of sounds, crowned by the chorale *come O death, thou brother of sleep*, in which, with astonishing boldness, *come and lead me forth*, death was intoned, glorified and desired so openly and, thanks to the slow, haunting bars of the music, lost its terror and was banished,

and even the sirens were drowned out, the ever louder drone of the bombers, the blasts of explosions and the collapsing of houses, the screams and the cries of the wounded, the grave tones of the Wehrmacht reports on the radio were drowned out and all the noise of the war,

so she wished for other, much louder chorales against death, chorales must ring out day and night, and all the stops of the organs must be pulled out until the war was over, and everybody must join in the singing at once, Schwester Ruth, Schwester Luise and she had to be just the start, everybody in her row, everybody in the church, the whole of Via Sicilia, the whole of Rome, the whole of Europe must join in and sing one chorale after the other without pause,

even the soldiers, as they had in the time of Frederick the Great, all generals on all fronts, Christians, heathens, Jews, communists, everybody must take a deep breath and join together in a monumental *Praise the Lord*, just as her father,

124

the captain, had sung it with such power, so that it would be impossible to do anything but join in at the top of one's voice and praise the *mighty King of all honour*,

           everything had its place beneath this heavenly canopy of music, even the wonderful stillness which descended with resonant vibrations at the end of the final bar, a detached, happy stillness which reflected her inner stillness, half a minute of silence, disturbed neither by applause nor restlessness, which corresponded with her happy silence and made her think that the loveliest thing in wartime was tranquility,

           and she resolved to write a letter that very evening, and to retain in her heart as much as possible of what she had seen on her walk and had felt beneath the heavenly vault of the music, and to relate it all to her beloved far away in Africa, today if possible, after supper, in a long letter.

Out 2010

"A mesmerising portrait ... it should be read." THE GUARDIAN
....

"... there's an understated power in Barbal's depiction of how the forces of history can shape the life of the powerless." FINANCIAL TIMES
....

"This is a small masterpiece." TLS

Out 2011

"Haunting, lyrical, wry, ironic – those are just a few of the notes struck with great originality by Matthias Politycki in his short novel."
ANTHEA BELL

....

"An intense reading experience ... Van Mersbergen tells what needs to be told and not a word more." DE MORGEN

....

"He is one of the best writers of his generation."
SÜDDEUTSCHE ZEITUNG

Peirene

Contemporary European Literature. Thought provoking, well designed, short.

"Two-hour books to be devoured in a single sitting: literary cinema for those fatigued by film." TLS

---

www.peirenepress.com

We love to hear your comments about the books.
E-mail the publisher directly at: meike.ziervogel@peirenepress.com